Ali,

I he

being in the middle!

BROCK

A FOUR SONS STORY

Dani René

xo

DANI RENÉ

Alli,

I hope you enjoy being in the middle!

To David
xo

I am strong, athletic, and son to a man I always wanted to be.
I had made plans, thought I was on that path, and then a
bullet stopped not just my father's heart, but mine too.

I've been living a life I'm not meant to.
I want more. I want to escape.
And I found someone who's given me a love
I never thought possible.

My name is Brock Pearson.

I am a free spirit who found happiness
in an unexpected place.
People assume I'll be another heir to our empire, but my
heart belongs elsewhere.

DEDICATION

To my Dirty Darklings who asked for two hot alphas to

devour. I hope you enjoy the ride!

───────PROLOGUE

B R O C K

TIME HAS PASSED.

Years even. But there's still a dull ache in my chest.

I attempt to shove the memories still haunting me to the darkest recesses of my mind. It's all I can do. My brothers go to a shrink for their issues.

Me?

I fuck.

I drink.

And I smoke the occasional joint.

I'm my father's son.

Eric fucking Pearson.

Watching them slowly move on with their lives makes me wonder if I'll ever get there. Nixon is all loved up with Rowan and Erica. Hayden has Katie and he's running Four Father's Freight. The only one who still gets me is my little brother Camden, but then again, he's younger.

Even though we've been through storms together, I needed to get away from the drama that seemed to follow the Pearson name back home. They didn't want me to leave, but I needed to move on, which is why I was all too happy to go away to college in California.

Hayden wasn't happy about me leaving home, or that I wanted to be so far away, but I'm not him. He's taken over the business, and I didn't want that for myself.

I miss my father. In the end, the four Pearson boys are still standing. After all the shit that went down when my dad was brutally murdered, I left. I fucking packed my bags and moved out. At first, just out of that horrible house that held such vicious memories, but then, when college started, I was gone for good.

Now, I live in a beautiful beach-view penthouse with my best friend—the one person I can always count on.

And he's the only one who knows me better than I know myself.

I glance up from my desk, watching the waves crash to the shore, spotting him with his surfboard, his shorts hanging low on his tapered hips. The tan, chiseled torso I've been in close contact with a few times since I've known him drips with the salty water from the ocean.

He makes his way up the beach toward the building where we live on the top floor. Having money offers certain privileges. And having fathers like ours—or in my case, *had*—means we are spoiled with luxuries other kids at school don't have. Where most kids are in cramped dorms, we're living better lives than men twice our age.

He lifts his head, finding my heated gaze on him, and offers a wave before disappearing from sight. In five minutes, he'll be walking through the door.

Before we get to what happens next. Before I tell you all about who I am, I need to introduce you to *him*. Even though I have four brothers, even though I had a father

I loved more than anything in this world and a mother who was killed before I even knew what affection was, *he* was in my story.

He was the one who stood by my side through my darkest days.

He was the one who saved me.

My best friend.

My savior.

Ethan Kingston.

ONE

E T H A N

THEY SAY THE APPLE DOESN'T FALL FAR FROM THE tree.

When it comes to me and my best friend, that saying is on point.

Brock and I are the bane of our professors' existence, but that doesn't matter. What does matter is we're the guys every girl at SoCal University wants to fuck, and it makes me smile whenever I think about it.

I've spent my life around a man I looked up to, my father, Levi Kingston, one of the most notorious playboy assholes in Florida. He used to fuck anything with a tight pussy and a set of tits—until he met my step-mom. Kristyn is gorgeous. The first time I was acquainted with her was a startling awakening. Her curves were on display when I walked into my childhood home to find her naked and all on show for me. My father definitely has great taste in women.

She's younger than him—much younger—but he's changed since he's been with her. The only time I ever recall him showing affection was with my mom. When she died, he became closed off. I was an angry teenager who blamed my dad for screwing things up, but deep down, I knew if he ever had the choice of having my mom back or living his life a bachelor, he'd choose her without a second thought.

Since the beautiful brunette burrowed her way into his life, he's the man I remember from my younger years. A caring, doting daddy with a baby who's been keeping him up all hours of the night. The kid has two loving parents, and I'm proud as hell to have a little sister to watch over.

I head into the kitchen, my mind still on Dad and Kristyn, and slam into a pretty blonde. Her big blue eyes are wide as she takes in my nearly naked body.

"Oh," she gasps, and my cock throbs in my tight briefs. A moment passes, but she doesn't drag her gaze away from my crotch.

"Not today, Blondie," I chuckle, gripping her upper arms and setting her closer to the door so I can get by to the coffee machine.

As soon as she's gone, I sigh, grab a mug, and fill it with some strong Colombian java. The place we have just off campus is perfect. With a view of the ocean and our own terrace that offers us space to barbeque and entertain friends from school, I've never been happier.

Brock and I decided to share an apartment when we moved out of our family homes and made our way west to study at the University of Southern California. He needed to get away from the shitstorm his family had been through, and I wanted my independence from my dad.

As I sip my coffee, I spy the little blonde heading out

without so much as a goodbye and know Brock must be passed out or nursing a hangover. Since we moved in together, things have been a roller coaster. After losing his dad two years ago, he's been working through a lot. Not so long ago, they had to deal with Brock's brother, Nixon's real dad showing up, and that's when Brock told me he doesn't think moving home after we graduate is what he wants.

I think he just enjoys the freedom L.A. gives. We surf whenever we have days off, get drunk, fuck pretty girls, and occasionally get stoned. Even though I've known him all my life, it was only when his dad got murdered by that dick, Jax Wheeler that I really got to know Brock Pearson. We quickly found a friendship around our love for partying and living with perpetual hangovers. Since Eric and my dad were best buddies, it was easy to see how Brock and I fell into the same routine.

Even though all the drama has died down surrounding the Pearsons, Brock is still adamant to live on the West

Coast after college. I think it's his preference to smoke weed and do vodka shots from the belly buttons of dancers in the local strip club.

Stalking into the hallway, I reach Brock's bedroom door and shove it wide open, hearing a groan in response. Leaning on the doorjamb, I watch him roll over onto his stomach. He's naked, his tan, toned body on display for the world to see. We've had our moments, a simple touch here, a slip of the hand there, but we've never been alone in those moments—never just us. And that's what I've been wanting.

Only...I don't know how to tell him or make a move.

"I told you to let yourself out," he mumbles into the pillow without looking up at me.

Lifting my mug, I take a sip of my coffee and chuckle.

He raises his head, and another groan follows a grunted, "Morning."

"You're going to be late." He doesn't have class for another hour, but he doesn't know what time it is, and I love to watch him squirm.

"Fuck you."

"You wish. Come on, B, we need to get going."

He mumbles another incoherent word, which I'm guessing is him cursing at me.

"Oh, and tell your bimbos to keep their eyes in their head next time they see my dick," I retort, offering him a side glance.

Brock moves quickly, shifting onto his ass. He sits on the edge of his bed and pins me with a glare. "Dude, she only looked at you because I was asleep and she probably wanted breakfast."

"I don't feed strays," I chuckle, stepping away from the doorway. "Now, come on. I don't feel like being late for Professor Chilton's class."

"Are we heading to that party tonight?" Brock questions before I exit his room.

I can't say no to him. We always have a good time, so I turn to my best friend and smirk. "As long as we're sharing dinner this time, I'm game."

His grin is devilish.

"Now we're talking." He shoves off the bed and heads into his adjoining bathroom, leaving me staring after him, unable to help admiring how his muscles flex as he moves. Shaking my head, I can't help smiling at the thought of sharing *dinner* with Brock again.

Like I said.

Like father, like son.

TWO ———————

B R O C K

EVEN THOUGH TIME HAS PASSED, I STILL FEEL IT. Anger.

Frustration.

And a whole lot of fucking sadness.

My head throbs like a fucking drum as I try to open my eyes and look at my reflection. The sun beats down on my chest from the open window overlooking the ocean beyond, the heat not helping my hangover. The constant thud feels like there's a heavy metal rhythm on repeat between my ears.

Thankfully, the blonde I fucked last night is gone. I don't need clingy one-night stands sticking around. They're better suited for a moment of fun. And she was far too squeaky for me to keep her around.

"Dude," the voice of my best friend comes from the doorway. "Are you done yet?"

"Yeah, yeah, I'm coming," I respond without looking at him. It's not the first time he's found me in this state. Normally, he'd be beside me, or curled around the girl between us, but today, he's on point with the tone of a serious student trying to get good grades.

The only difference between us and the rest of the fucking student body is our money ensures we're part of the more elite squad. Since Levi, Ethan's dad, makes hefty donations to the university, the same way my Dad used to in order to keep Hayden out of trouble, they've given us free reign on campus to not only miss classes if we choose to, but own the whole fucking college. At least Ethan isn't sleeping with the professors like my dear old brother used to.

Yeah, I get good grades. My GPA is perfect, I study my ass off, and Ethan knows it, but he likes to tell me off when I'm acting like an asshole. I blame that on my father.

"Quit bugging me. You know I'll get my ass ready," I groan, pulling the towel from the rack and hanging it closer to the shower. I know he won't leave me alone. He'll stand there like a wounded puppy until I move my ass.

As much as he frustrates me when he's in this mood, Ethan Kingston is my best friend and the only one who understands me. Since Dad took a fatal bullet, I may have gone off the deep end a few times.

Fuck it.

I practically live hanging off the edge of a cliff by one finger. One day, something is going to push me off and I'll tumble to the rocks below. Stepping into the shower, I turn on the taps and let the cold water jolt me into action. The smell of the cinnamon soap I use fills the space, and I quickly wash off, knowing I'll soon have my best friend at the door if I spend too much time in here.

As soon as I'm back in the bedroom, I feel his eyes on me. I tug a pair of briefs up my thighs. Turning to meet

Ethan's dark eyes, I offer him a cocky wink before pulling on a t-shirt.

"You smell better than you did this morning with the smell of that blonde's pussy all over you," he chuckles, taunting me.

"Get out of my fucking room, dude, unless you want a piece of this?" I grab my crotch, and we both laugh.

"It's the other way around, man, you just want a piece of mine."

I chuck the pillow at him, which he easily catches and lobs back, thumping me right on the back of my head.

"Your ugly ass needs to be in class. We have an exam today," he says, spinning on the heel of his fancy sneakers.

Ethan is the artsy one, with a love of surfing and painting rather than the corporate shit his father does for a living. It's been a sore point between the two of them for years. After Levi Kingston met Kristyn, he calmed down somewhat. Now that they have a kid, he's changed a lot since the days of he and my dad hitting on every female within a five-mile radius.

One thing I can say about one of my dad's best friends is he has amazing taste in pussy. The woman is nothing short of a supermodel. And when she was pregnant not so long ago, she looked even more attractive. *Who the fuck knew?*

Shoving the pillow away, I tug on a pair of jeans and make my way into the kitchen to find Ethan at the counter drinking coffee. Even though we do argue, there's something so much more between us—something I never knew existed. He's brought me out of the darkness that consumed me.

The images that ran through my mind at night, every time I closed my eyes, haunted me. Seeing my father's lifeless body staring back at me was enough to send me over the edge, but it was Ethan who was beside me. He calmed the erratic emotions that attacked me.

Anger, frustration, and rage consumed me for weeks after. So much so, I wanted to hit anything in my path, throw my fist through a goddamn window, but with Ethan's guidance, I focused my anger on a punching bag instead of a wall.

He dragged my broody ass to the gym daily. Without complaining, without so much as an uttered judgment, he was right there with every episode. That's when we first started sharing women. When I needed a release, he'd invite anything with a set of tits and lithe long legs to his place. The Kingston house was my sanctuary, and now, my sanctuary is here.

But it's more than that. Ethan was there for everything I overcame. He was there to ease the agony.

At times, I still go there, still feel the depression threatening to overtake me, but Ethan remains my savior. I feel his eyes on me, but he stays quiet, and I head straight for the coffee. Three things we always have in our shared apartment:

Coffee.

Beer.

Pussy.

Isn't that what you're meant to do in college—party your days away until you're supposed to get a full-time job and act like an adult?

"What's up your ass today?" I ask, filling a mug before meeting his dark eyes. He looks exactly like Levi—the epitome of tall, dark, and fucking handsome. Girls practically fall over themselves to get his attention.

"Nothing. Get your shit together, Brock," he bites out, and I'm tempted to tell him to go fuck himself. But knowing Ethan, he'll probably retort with some snarky comment.

"This is my life," I remind him. "I can do whatever the fuck I want with my shit." We're at a standoff. It's not the first time we've butted heads about my partying. He has no say over my life and what I do with it, but I know he's only looking out for me.

Our friendship runs deeper than I ever thought. I never wanted anyone in my corner. My heart ceased to beat when my father's did. Even though I'm close to my brothers, losing my dad hurt more than I ever could have imagined. It was a pain so severe, it stole my will to move on.

He was an asshole.

But I loved him fiercely.

And as much as I want to deny that, I don't, because as angry as I was at him for how he went about taking Rowan as his own, I could never hate him. And now I'm here with no one to be angry with, so Ethan is the one who takes the brunt of my shit. Thankfully, he hasn't walked out yet.

THREE

E T H A N

SOMETIMES I WONDER HOW I'VE PUT UP WITH Brock's reckless attitude and anger for so long. Given the choice, I'd do it again, but I wish he'd see how much he has going for him and stop drinking himself into oblivion.

When my mother died, my father practically slapped some sense into me when I wanted to spend more time on the beach surfing than going to school. But with my best friend, it's different. He witnessed his father's brutal death, had the pregnant neighbor take a bullet to the stomach, and then, to make matters worse, learned his mother hadn't run off and had been buried a few feet away from the swimming pool we spent most days in. The shit that went down at the Pearson residence was fucked up.

Our friendship means a lot to me, even though I'll never tell the asshole that to his face. He's far too arrogant for his own good already. Like father, like son. But I care about him, perhaps more than I should or care to admit. Over the past few years, feelings have changed between us. There's much more between me and Brock than either of us have been willing to admit.

"I'm ready," he stalks out of his bedroom, looking like he's about to head to a photoshoot. With his tan skin, blue eyes, and that dark hair, he looks more like Eric every day—a playboy in the making.

"Let's get out of here," I tell him, rising from the sofa and grabbing my keys. We don't live far from campus, but I prefer driving. That way, I can offer a ride to a certain beauty I've had my eye on for a couple weeks now. Her pert, round ass looks good enough to eat as she sways her hips on campus. And it's not just me who's noticed. Every male in the vicinity has seen her. A smile that lights up the whole goddamn world makes me want to see it on her face all the time. If Brock knew I was salivating over her every day, he'd give me grief, and this is why I've kept it to myself. For now.

I follow Brock down to the Jeep sitting in my parking space. Once the engine roars to life, he turns on the stereo, notching the volume up to almost max, and I wonder what happened to the hangover. Unless he popped a couple painkillers. I don't ask. Instead, I take in the boom of the rock music from the speakers as I weave us through traffic toward school.

"Who the hell is that?" Brock questions as I pull into a parking spot close to the building. I turn off the engine and drag my gaze over to where he's gesturing with his chin.

Fuck.

"A pretty little thing I've been keeping my eye on for the past few weeks," I tell him, a smirk curling my lips. "What do you think?" I cast my glance at Brock who's eyeing her up.

"Not bad. Not bad at all, man," he chuckles.

The girl in question is petite, dressed in a pair of ripped faded blue jeans that hug her slim thighs. Her top is white, tight-fitting, and offers an intoxicating view of her tits. Smooth caramel skin hints at a natural tan, and when she turns around, I'm afforded a glimpse of the ass I've been picturing in front of me as I fuck her from behind.

"Dude," Brock grits out, "are you getting a boner next to me?" He chuckles, and I swat at his chest.

"Fuck off, Pearson," I retort. "That ass would look so good on my dick," I tell him, still in awe of the woman with the long, wild, chocolate curls I want to fist in my grip.

"We can share," my best friend says, and my gaze snaps to his. Those blue eyes that match all the Pearson boys flit with satisfaction and mischief. When it comes to women and alcohol, Brock is the first one in line. And he can score pussy like a world-famous quarterback.

"Sounds like a plan. She's a junior, though," I respond. "She's probably been warned off us seniors." I turn my attention back to the girl who's stolen my focus. Everything about her screams innocence—something my father taught me to always want in a woman. When I asked him why, he told me it's to ensure you're the one to corrupt her, and even though she may go off and fuck other guys, you'll always be the one who was there first.

"Let's go," Brock says. He's out of the car in seconds, but I don't move. I watch him saunter up to the girl with a swagger that tells me he's feeling far too confident. There's something about her that makes me think she's not going to fall for his shit.

I can't hear them, but her body language alone is icy at best. He turns, heading away from the beauty without casting me a glance. My phone vibrates with a message, and when I glance at the screen, I see his name.

Laughing, I open the app and find his message.

She's hard work. Your turn, Smooth Talker Kingston.

With pleasure, I think to myself.

Exiting the vehicle, I make my way to where she's still standing, holding a stack of books and looking around as if she's lost. It doesn't take me long to reach her, and when I do, the smell of coconut and the ocean emanate from her. My two favorite things.

"A surfer," I say as soon as she turns her big blue eyes to me. They're luminous against her tan skin. She's exotic looking, and I'm dying to get a taste.

"And you know this how?" she sasses, turning her full attention on me.

Shrugging, I take her in, from her bright yellow flip flops to her luxurious curls. "You're dressed for the beach for one." I point to her casual attire. "And you smell like coconut and the sea. Two of my favorite things." My assessment makes her smile, and I'm stunned at how much more beautiful she is when she gifts me a glimpse of her happiness.

"So, you love the waves as well?" She crinkles her nose as she glances up at me, the sun glinting off her gold necklace and a small dolphin charm hanging between her cleavage.

"I have an affinity for them, yeah."

"And your friend?" She tips her head toward the path Brock took only moments ago. "Does he always try to pick up chicks with bad one liners?"

"Only when he's hungover." I can't help chuckling.

She's sweet, innocent, but there's a snarky sass that makes me want to delve so much deeper and learn who this beauty is. When I look at her now, I don't see a girl—I see a woman who's got a good sense of self.

"Well, tell him he shouldn't be attempting that when he's been drinking. It's not attractive." Her words cause another laugh to rumble in my chest.

"Tell me your name and I'll reacquaint you with

Brock." I point to my best friend, who's leaning against a tree, his shades covering his blue eyes.

"Camila," she responds, a hint of an accent peeking through. She's foreign, or something. Explains her exotic beauty. Most girls who follow us around are blonde dolls caked in thick eyeliner, even thicker concealer, and have fake everything because they have far too much money to splurge on attempting to look perfect.

But when I look at Camila, I don't see anything that needs covering up. She's perfect as she is. I see beauty in her conventional casual clothes, and the fact that she has no makeup on. It's refreshing, it's different, and my cock agrees, throbbing at the sight of her smile.

A beauty spot sits just on the apple of her left cheek. The gentle curve of her small button nose crinkles when she grins, which makes her plump, full lips shimmer with the light dusting of clear gloss on them. A normal girl in an overly fake world.

"Where are you from, sweetheart?"

"Here. Well, my father moved here from Spain when I was ten," she informs me, a soft smile on her lips. Her eyes shine as she looks up at me.

"What's your name?" she asks, snapping me out of the filthy thoughts of what she could wrap those lips around.

"Ethan," I offer, holding out my hand. She accepts with a smile.

"Nice to meet you, Ethan." The way her accent caresses my name makes me bite back a groan of want and need. This woman may just kill me by whimpering my name. "You going to introduce me to your friend now?"

I nod. "Come. He's not as bad as you may think he is."

FOUR

B R O C K

I WATCH HIM FLIRT AND CAN'T HELP SMILING. WHEN I saw her, I offered up the option of sharing, and if I know anything, it's that my best friend can't refuse a threesome with a beautiful woman.

It started one night without us planning it. The chemistry was there, and I went with it. We're young, experimenting, and I enjoy it—so does he. My brothers have their assumptions about my sexuality. I know they do, but they've overcomplicated something that's pretty simple.

I never denied there's something between Ethan and I, even though we've never said it out loud. It's always been there, and with time, it's only become more obvious. Yes, we like to fuck the same woman at the same time, but we've never ventured further than that. Not on our own.

If something ever happened between us and we ended up in bed together, or on the sofa, or anywhere, for that matter, I wouldn't say no. I'd definitely be down for it.

When he saunters toward the building with her beside him, I know it's in the bag. My head is still pounding as they near me, but I blink away the violent hangover and offer her a smile.

"Hi." I smirk, watching her tan skin turn a darker shade with the blush on her cheeks.

She offers a hand to me, greeting in a gentle tone. "Hello."

"I'm the asshole," I tell her, taking her hand in mine, lifting it to my lips and pressing a kiss to her knuckles. "But you'll get used to me."

"Where is your next class?" Ethan rolls his eyes at me, then drags his gaze over to her. He's intrigued by her beauty, overly so.

"Um..." she mumbles, opening a schedule. "Art History." Her eyes glimpse my way, lingering over me before lifting to my stare.

"Good," I respond first. "Ethan, let's walk the gorgeous lady to her class." I offer her my arm, which she accepts after a moment's hesitation.

With Ethan on her left and me on her right, we lead her into the large building where we find students milling around. She tells us about her love of the ocean, how she came here to study and surf, and I can't help smiling when I think about her tight little body in a swimsuit.

"You'll have to come to one of our pool parties," I offer, casting my eyes to my best friend.

He nods. "We normally have them once a month," he explains as we stop outside her classroom. "Your first class." Ethan offers her one of his charming grins.

"This is it?" She looks almost nervous. Her innocence is like a drug I'm dying to taste.

"We'll see you later, yeah?" Ethan smiles. He's always been so laid back, and girls love it.

"That sounds nice. Bye, Brock. Bye, Ethan." She waves shyly and leaves us staring at her pert ass in those tight blue jeans.

"Jesus, the things I want to do to that ass," I grin, my cock already throbbing at the thought of sliding between her cheeks.

"Come on, man." Ethan tugs me toward our classroom, and away from the pretty vixen I'm dying to get a taste of. "You're a manwhore," my best friend chuckles.

"Yeah? Didn't hear you complaining the last time we—"

"Brock," a sultry voice comes from behind me, and I shudder. I'd recognize that sickly tone anywhere. The blonde sidles up between me and Ethan, hooking her arms through ours and entering class with us. Unfortunately, I made the mistake of taking her home one night, and now, she's always hanging around. We met in one of the bars downtown while I was looking to get my dick wet. She, on the other hand, is looking for a ring on her dainty little finger. *Not happening, sweetheart.*

Ethan tugs himself free, leaving me to deal with my mistake.

"Look, Monique—"

"It's Lauren," she bites out, planting her hands on her hips as if she's about to admonish me. The corner of my mouth kicks up into an amused grin. *Fuck this.*

"Lauren, we're not together and we'll never be together, so just quit trying, sweetheart," I inform her, keeping my tone low, hoping like hell I'm making myself clear.

"You don't have to be an asshole," she huffs, her cheeks turning bright pink. My gaze falls to her fake pouty lips and I can't help the revulsion that trickles through me. She reminds me of the women my dad used to fuck—fake Barbie dolls. As much as I don't want to be like my Dad, I always end up in bed with those fake, clingy girls. I don't realize it 'til I wake up the next morning and regret every moment. And those times, I just wish I had the real thing—a real woman who can hold an intelligent conversation.

"Trust me, sweetheart, I do. I am an asshole. So, I would suggest you turn on your fuck-me heels and leave me the hell alone." No more words are spoken. She twirls in what I'm guessing is meant to be seductive, but is far from it, and I can't help shaking my head. I'm in my seat beside Ethan when I feel his gaze on me. "What?"

"Nothing."

"Don't give me that shit. Say what you want to say." Dragging my gaze to his, I meet his dark brown eyes.

He shrugs, twirling his pencil through his fingers. "You know you're just like him. You sometimes lose focus on who you are."

His words slam into my chest.

He's right.

"Fuck you, Ethan."

"Later." He smirks as our professor strolls into class, and my chest tightens in anticipation that he would be down for something happening between us as well. My cock throbs in my jeans at the thought. Facing the front, I attempt to calm myself, but I know nothing will clear my mind of the thoughts now racing around my head.

FIVE

ETHAN

THE SUN BEATS DOWN ON MY BACK AS I WADE through the crystal-clear water, my mind filled with thoughts of our new conquest—Camila. Brock is definitely interested, and I certainly am, so we need to find a way to get her between us.

Most girls we've shared were looking for it. They didn't care that they had us both—it was exactly what they wanted—but I have a feeling Camila is different. She'll need coaxing. Perhaps a date with each of us before we drop her into the deep end of the ocean.

I think about Dad and how he and Eric would go out and find pretty girls to share. I'd been in the house a couple times when they had brought the parties back to the mansion. At the time, I was angry at him, but I can't deny he and Eric had some fun with the women who fell for their one liners. He thinks I had no idea, but there were many times I heard some woman squealing from down the hall, and the next morning, I would "accidentally" stumble into one of the young women in our kitchen. I always wondered if he'd ever find *the one* again.

Which brings me back to my feelings. I haven't yet told him about Brock. At least, I haven't told anyone I'm bi. Dad wouldn't care. He's not the type to disown me over something so trivial, but I need to tell him, because each day I'm here, living with my best friend, I realize my feelings run far deeper than I expected. Even though Brock and I haven't taken that step physically, I hope we will.

There are times I wish my father wasn't such an asshole while I was growing up. Times where I wonder what would've happened if my mother lived, if she would've made him more of a dad rather than a drill sergeant. I still remember when she was around, how she'd make him smile.

Those times were my favorite.

Even though Kristyn kicked his ass into gear, I didn't think he'd change, but with my baby sister, Brynn, he's become the dad I remember once more. He's spending a lot more time at home, which is a good sign. But I haven't been home in a while, which I'll need to rectify soon. Problem is, I need to broach the subject with Brock.

"What the fuck are you daydreaming about?" *Speak of the devil.*

"I was thinking about beating your ass on this wave," I shout as I lie front first on my board, my arms working hard to get me closer. I'm up and on my feet in seconds, as soon as it crests, and Brock is right beside me, riding the wave.

This is where he's more himself than anywhere else.

His eyes shine with happiness. He's carefree and relaxed. And it makes me happy. When we reach the shore, I stay on my board, my legs hanging over either edge as he turns to regard me. "Are we heading to Kula?"

The place is a little shack not far from where we're surfing. When he offers me a grin, the one I know far too well, I nod. He has something on his mind.

We make our way, dripping wet, toward the small café. After shoving the tip of our boards in the sand, I follow him up to the counter where he orders two coconut waters and two plates of fries.

Once we're seated, I wonder if it's time to ask him about heading home for a weekend. We have a break coming up, and seeing the rest of the family will be good, not only for him, but me too. My dad mentioned Hayden wanted to have a get-together at some point soon.

"I've been thinking," I start, lifting the bottle and taking a long swig, "we should head home for a little while." My words stop Brock from taking a long gulp of his drink. "Just for a weekend or something," I offer. "I want us to talk to my dad, and we need to talk to your brothers."

"Yeah," he responds finally. "We can head back in a couple weeks, but I don't know if telling them I want to live here permanently, with you, is a good idea."

"Why? We're friends. Aren't we?" I question.

He shrugs. "I don't know if they'll accept it, the situation."

"We're a situation, Brock?"

"No, I mean...fuck, I just don't want them to be angry, or some shit. You know? Hayden wasn't happy I wanted to go to school so far from home and if I lived here permanently..." his voice tapers off, and I know exactly what he means—we'd finally have to talk about our emotions or what's going on between us, because there is definitely something between us. He glances at me, his eyes holding all the emotion he's feeling—that I'm feeling.

"Two plates of fries," a familiar sweet voice comes toward our table, interrupting the conversation. We both glance up, and there in a white apron is our beauty from this morning. "Oh, hi." She smiles, making my chest ache. When I glance over at Brock, he's grinning from ear to ear.

"Baby girl," he coos, "aren't you looking damn fine in that." His blue eyes roam over her slight form appreciatively, and I can't help smiling. This exotic beauty has definitely caught his attention.

"Eat your fries," she sasses, placing the bowls on the table in front of each of us. We both watch her stroll away, her hips swaying only slightly, and I wonder if she's enjoying making our cocks hard. Because I know mine definitely is.

"We need to get her between us," he tells me, turning to meet my darkened gaze. My brow arches up at his insistence. "What? Jealous?" he quips. If there were ever a time I'd be jealous, this isn't it.

"You're a dick," I tell him, popping a fry into my mouth.

"You love my dick," he quips as he drowns his lunch

in ketchup.

"And you love mine, so we're square," I retort with a smirk.

He shrugs in agreement before devouring his fries. The unspoken desire between us is at an all-time high. Perhaps I should make the move. If I did it, the pressure would be off. Our playful banter is no longer just fun, it's become more.

———

We didn't see Camila again before leaving the café, and I should've asked if she lives close by. The party we're planning is this weekend, and I want to make sure she's there. My phone buzzes, dragging my attention away from the project I'm working on.

Levi.

"Hey, Dad," I greet after accepting the call.

"How's school?" he questions gruffly, and I wonder if the company is causing him a lack of sleep. Or if there's something else bothering him, then I realize what's coming up soon—the anniversary of my mother's death.

Sighing, I lean back in my chair and respond. "Fine. We're thinking of heading home in a couple weeks, as soon as we get a break."

"I think you should," he says. "I know Kristyn would like to see you, and Brynn needs to remember what her brother looks like." They were torn between names just before Kristyn gave birth, but as soon as she arrived, the name Brynn stuck out. It has a nice ring to it. *Brynn Kingston*. She's only six months old, and she's already got my father wrapped around her little finger.

I nod because I miss the little munchkin. "Yeah. I'll bring her something from the store down the road. I'll ask Kristyn what she needs."

"Good," Dad grumbles. "How is Brock?" His tone softens. I'm sure everyone back home thinks we're a couple, or at least suspect it.

"He's okay. You know, still an asshole."

"Watch your mouth, and no cursing around Brynn

when you get here," he bites out, ever the loving daddy.

"She's a baby, she doesn't—"

"You will respect her and Kristyn," he retorts. Jesus, my dad can be a dick sometimes.

"Yeah, I know, Dad."

"Say hi to Brock," he tells me. "Let me know when you're coming so I can make sure the spare room is set up for him."

"I will. Bye, Dad." I hang up, knowing he meant to say Kristyn will ensure everything is ready for our visit. As soon as Eric was murdered, and they'd found Brock's mother's body in their backyard, my best friend practically moved into our house. He lived there for so long, he became part of our family.

I turn my attention back to the screen to focus. If this shit isn't done, I'll get a bad grade, and that's the last thing I need to hear Levi complain about.

SIX

BROCK

"**S**O, WE'RE EACH GOING ON A DATE WITH HER?" I ask Ethan after he tells me his plan. Granted, I have to agree. She's not like the normal girls we bring home, so perhaps he has a point.

"I think it will make her feel more comfortable with us, and then gently nudge her into the direction of a threesome," he says, sounding as though he's planned this out.

"And I go first?" He nods. "Okay." Shrugging, I head down the steps as he makes his way to the Jeep. The quad is packed with students, but I see her through the crowd. Once I reach Camila, I tap her on the shoulder, and she jumps. "Hey, baby girl, just me." I offer a smirk, and she blushes.

"Hey, I thought you left already," she tells me.

"No, we had a test to finish up." My explanation is met with a nod. "Listen, I was thinking, we should have dinner, at our place?" I know it's not what Ethan suggested, but I formulated another plan. Instead of doing this separately, she should get used to us together.

"Sure, when?"

"Tonight? Me, you, and Ethan," I tell her, pointing to the Jeep. I can feel my best friend's eyes on me, burning into me. "We'd like to get to know you."

"It sounds nice. Text me the address," she tells me with one of those bright smiles, her eyes gleaming with excitement.

"Sure will, sweetheart." I lean in, placing a gentle kiss on her cheek, reveling in her smooth skin. As soon as I slip into the seat beside Ethan, he turns to me, but before he can say anything, I explain, "I decided a quiet dinner with us both is better."

"Perhaps you're right," he offers, starting the car. I

can't hide the shock on my face. At times, we've butted heads over my methods, but right now, I'm grinning like an idiot because he actually agrees with me.

"Are you making dinner?" I ask, watching him from the corner of his eye. His hand rests casually on the steering wheel, his other on his thigh, tapping to the music.

"Yeah. What do you want?" He chuckles. "Think if I make some pasta she'll be impressed and offer us that sweet body?"

"Ha! You're sounding more and more like me all the time," I chuckle.

"If you can't beat 'em, join 'em," he responds, casting one of his heated gazes on me before turning his attention back to the road. We're pulling up to the apartment when my phone rings. I glance at the screen and Hayden's name flashes at me.

"Hey," I answer, pressing the phone to my ear.

"Brock," my brother says in a tone that matches my

father's. Since he's taken over the company, he's changed somewhat, and that's why I never wanted to do it. I never saw myself in a suit and tie every day sitting behind a desk.

"How are you?"

"Good. I was wondering when you were planning on coming home again," he says easily. "I'm planning a family get together and I'm sure Erica misses you. Nixon and Rowan say she's saying a few words here and there. They were excited when she said what sounded like your name." At the mention of my little sister's name, my heart expands with love. She's incredible. I never thought I'd ever be comfortable around her because of my father and Rowan's relationship. There was a certain tension about them being together. But Erica is innocent in all the shit, and I could never blame her for Dad's misgivings.

"Actually," I tell him, glancing beside me into dark eyes, "Ethan and I were planning on coming down soon."

"You and Ethan?" The way he questions me tells

me he suspects something my best friend and I already know. There's more between us than just friendship.

The corner of Ethan's mouth kicks into a knowing grin. He places a hand on my thigh, stroking it slowly. Shaking my head, I clear my throat and attempt to focus.

"Yeah. We wanted to come home," I choke out as my best friend's hand finds my crotch. My jeans are becoming unbearably tight when he squeezes my cock through the material, causing a groan to rumble in my chest. My heart thuds against my ribs as desire burns through me, heating my blood causing my dick to harden. Sure, we've touched on occasion when we've taken girls to bed, but this is the first time it's just us.

Of course, being Ethan, he'd choose the exact moment I'm on the phone with my brother to make a move. He is making a move, right? Or is he fucking with me? I turn my glare on him, swatting his hand away, but his response is a quiet chuckle.

He doesn't look at me directly, and I'm sure he's just

messing with me, until he finally meets my stare. Ethan's dark eyes burn with lust. For me. My cock jolts in his grip at the hunger in his gaze.

"Okay. Bring Ethan to dinner," Hayden says calmly—a little too calm. He knows. I know he knows. My brother is not stupid.

"Yeah, sure. He'll love that," I tell him while Ethan massages my rock-solid cock through the material separating me and his hand. My mind whirls while I try to focus on the conversation with my brother.

Fuck, we're doing this. He's doing this. There's no screwing around. My best friend is stroking my dick through my shorts and there's not a woman in sight.

"When is Cam coming here?" I ask, hoping to get the details of my little brother's visit in an attempt to distract my growing desire.

"He's flying out in a couple weeks for some debate competition in SoCal. I'll text you the date so he can hang out at your place, or stay over. Is that good for you?"

Hayden takes on a formal tone when he talks about the other siblings. He's had to grow up too fast, taking care of the rest of us and the business before he ever got a chance to live his life.

"Sounds good. I'll pick him up from the airport," I respond to my brother. "I have to go," I bite out as Ethan's mouth finds the lobe of my ear, biting down hard. Dropping my phone in the console, I turn my attention to him, grip the dark hair at the nape of his neck, and bring his mouth to mine. Our lips hover so close, the heat of our breaths mixing together, and for a moment, everything is still. He waits for me to make the next move, offering me a second to stop this, but I can't. I want this. I want him. There's no rethinking the path we're on.

I've never been so sure of anything in my life.

With a groan, I move those few inches toward him, meeting him the rest of the way, eager for the line we're about to cross.

Our lips mold together, heat searing through me, his

hand still jerking me off while my free one finds his hard shaft. Heat burns through me, wild and incinerating. So quickly, he brings me to the point where I feel like I may explode. Nobody has ever had such an intense effect on me.

"I'm going to fucking lose it," I growl, and his tongue dips into my mouth as mine duels back with equal ferocity.

We're just mouths, and hands, and tongues, and I thank God we're parked underground so nobody can see us. A deep growl vibrates through Ethan's chest when I suck his hot tongue hard, biting down and dragging my teeth along the length.

Goddamn, we're doing this. We're finally doing this.

"Taking this upstairs?" I hiss when he squeezes my steel shaft hard through my jeans. My balls tighten with the need to release.

"Fuck yes," he growls like an animal, and we're out of the car and in the elevator. I don't know what's gotten into him, but I'm not complaining.

SEVEN

E T H A N

WE REACH THE APARTMENT, AND I'M ALREADY tugging my shirt off. Brock's is on the floor in the next second, and then I'm pressed against the wall beside our door, his toned chest, chiseled abs, and smooth skin against mine.

Finally. Fucking finally.

The heat of his kiss burns me right down to my soul. I know it. I've always known it, but never admitted it. I've only ever allowed myself to think about it. I knew one of us had to make the move. And I decided it would be me. Why I chose to do it while he was talking to his brother is beyond me, but I did it, and he didn't push me away. His frown, that tension that knots his muscles made me want to see him smile, and the only thing I could think about was touching him, feeling him hard in my hand.

We've fucked around before with a chick between us, but this is different. I want him. Alone. Just the two of us. As his hands trail down each dip and peak of my chest and stomach, I realize I've always wanted him and nothing is going to change that.

"This is—"

"It is." His hands find my belt, undoing it and *me* in the process. I'm no longer confused at what I want. I know he will always be in my life. Once the leather is pulled free from my jeans, I get to work on his, tugging it from the loops and dropping it on the floor with a loud clank.

"Brock," I breathe, inhaling him as he stands before me, both our jeans undone. We're a mess, filled with need and hunger. "This isn't a threesome, a fuck, a one-night stand."

"No," he agrees with a nod. "It's our lives."

"You want this?" I shove my jeans down and step

out of them, but don't drop my gaze. I'm locked on him. My cock is thick and hard in my boxers, ready for something—for him.

He removes his jeans easily, allowing them to pool on the floor, and I watch as he steps out of them.

"I've always wanted this," he affirms, affection and lust both present in his heated gaze. My chest aches, squeezing with emotion at his confession. I've only ever admitted it to myself, that I've wanted it too. It feels right, and I nod.

Brock steps closer to me. We're two men who need each other—two boys who grew together as one—and now, we're taking a step we'll never be able to go back from. And I never want to go back.

Dropping to my knees, I tug Brock's briefs down and take in his hard cock, never wanting something so bad in my life. My hand grips him firmly, and I start moving slowly, up and down, jerking my best friend. Arousal glistens on the tip, and I lean in to lap at him—something

I've never done before.

The salty juice coats my tongue as I suck him into my mouth, taking it slow. My gaze darts up to his, meeting those blue orbs. I take him deeper, reveling in his silky hardness on my tongue. A groan from Brock rumbles down toward me, his eyes shining with unrestrained desire. I've seen him fuck, I've seen him make woman scream his name, but this...it's so much more.

"Touch yourself," he pleads, his voice raspy and dripping with the seduction he normally offers the girls who smile at him. My hand fists my cock, stroking it, feeling him and me throb with pleasure.

I move my mouth up and down, faster and faster, until he grips my hair, holding me steady. Allowing my mouth to pop off his cock, he smirks down at me and shakes his head.

"My turn," he offers, and I rise, leaning back against the wall once more. Brock drops to his knees, and his hot mouth engulfs my dick. My balls tighten, and I almost come in his mouth, but breathe through the sensation. Everything about this moment feels far too good. His lips around shaft. His eyes gazing up at me. His lean body kneeling before me. The sight is otherworldly. It's fucking intense. I've never experienced this before. No girl has made my body shudder with need as much as he does.

"Brock."

"In my mouth," he utters, then works me into his throat. Blue eyes glisten, and I can't hold back. My body overrules my mind as I shoot jet after jet of release into my best friend's mouth.

He swallows every fucking drop before rising to his full height, and I take my turn again, swallowing as much of him into my throat as I can. My hand jerking the base of his cock, I watch in awe as he finds euphoria, grunting in pleasure.

The line between what we've had and what we've so clearly wanted has been blurred. Brock and I took a step we can never go back from. My chest is tight with emotion, with elation, and I don't know what we'll do next. But I can't fucking wait.

EIGHT ————

C A M I L A

AS I NEAR THE APARTMENT, THERE ARE BUTTERFLIES in my stomach. They're alive and attacking with a vengeance. I'm not sure what they expect, or what they have planned, but I find myself eager to know more about both of them.

My hands are shaking, palms sweaty. It sounds cliché, but all the emotions both Brock and Ethan have stirred in me have me trembling. I've heard rumors about them. When I mentioned Brock's name to one of my classmates, she said they have a reputation of sharing girls, and I wonder if that's what they want with me.

I talked myself into coming here because I like them. I haven't been on many dates. Hell, I've only had two boyfriends—one when I was sixteen and the other only a year ago when I turned eighteen. We dated for a few months before we broke it off.

When I think about Brock and Ethan however, I find myself grinning like an idiot, like I'm excited to be venturing on a path I never thought I'd take. Something new and different. Wondering how it would work with them both, I inhale deeply attempting to calm my nerves, which doesn't help at all, I doubt anything can at this stage.

Guys have not been on my radar because I wanted to focus on school, but I want to also have fun and enjoy my time here. Who's to say I can't have it all? At first, I thought I liked Ethan, but then Brock swooped in, and now I'm confused. I like them both. And it seems they're okay with that.

I guess, why choose if I can have both?

Does that make me greedy?

Perhaps.

I lift my hand and press the buzzer to their

apartment. As soon as the door opens, I'm breathless. Ethan is dressed in a plain green t-shirt and a pair of blue jeans that make him look relaxed, yet sexy. His dark hair is styled back, showing off his dark eyes. There are times his hair falls into his left eye, making him seem more innocent than I'm sure he is.

"Hey," he greets, taking my hand and leading me into their apartment.

"Wow." A gasp of shock falls from my lips. The place is amazing. The modern furniture, along with the white and gray color scheme make the space seem huge, but it's the wall of windows overlooking the ocean that does it.

"Yeah, it's our own little piece of heaven," Ethan tells me proudly. I follow him into the living room where I take in the black sofas and red shag carpet under a glass coffee table. Who knew guys could be so tidy?

"Yeah, I can see why," I tell him.

I turn to find him staring at me. The dress I chose is thigh-length, black, and it hugs my skinny frame. I've always been shy of my body. I'm not built like most of the girls with my slim waist and small breasts. But there's an appreciation in Ethan's gaze that makes me blush.

"You look amazing," he finally murmurs, stepping closer to me. My stomach does a tumble when he lifts my chin with his index finger. He doesn't lean in, he doesn't kiss me, just offers me a smile.

Someone clears their throat, and I take a step backward, startled. When I turn around, I find Brock inches from me, a wolfish smile on his lips.

"Start the party without me?" he quips, leaning in, his mouth is so close to mine, but not touching.

"Not just yet," Ethan answers for me, calming the storm that seems to be brewing between the three of us. It's clear they both want this—want me. "We're glad you came tonight."

"Thank you," I offer the dark-eyed man a smile. Because that's what he is, a man. They both are.

His hands find purchase on my hips and he tugs me

closer. His lips find mine in a gentle, yet searing kiss. His tongue asks for entry with a gentle probe, and I give it to him.

I've wanted to kiss him since he walked up to me a couple days ago, but nothing could've prepared me for the butterflies wildly fluttering in my stomach. He tastes like soda and candy—and I want so much more.

"Tell me this is okay?" Ethan questions, his gaze pleading with me.

I nod, and that's all he needs. Ethan's hands remain on my hips as Brock's strong hand cups my cheek and his lips land on mine, kissing me as deeply as Ethan did. It's heady being between two strong men. It's so far outside my comfort zone, I feel dizzy when he finally pulls away.

"Let's eat," Ethan announces, and the look in both their gazes tells me they're not thinking about food at this point. He leaves us in the living room and heads into the kitchen. The sound of dishes being manhandled echoes through the space as he gets the dinner table ready.

Brock's hand trails its way over my arm, dragging my attention to him. With a crooked smile, he tells me, "If anything ever feels uncomfortable, you tell us, okay?"

"I will."

"Promise?" He's serious, so damn serious, and it makes my heart race.

"I promise, I'll tell you and Ethan."

He nods, planting a kiss on my forehead, then laces his fingers with mine. We follow the noise in the kitchen to find Ethan finishing up something on the stove. When he turns to me, he offers a wink before I'm seated by Brock.

Moments later, we're all at the table, plates full, and two sets of eyes on me.

"Tell us about you," Ethan says, a curious glint in his eyes.

"Well, I have a sister, and I'm not exactly the outgoing type, so I spend most of my time reading or surfing," I start, piling my fork with pasta before putting it in my mouth. When the flavors hit my tongue, I can't help moaning in pleasure. "This is amazing."

"I figured out how to cook when I was growing up," Ethan tells me. "My mother..." his words taper off, and I have a feeling he's going to tell me something bad. "She died when I was younger," he continues after taking a sip of the soda beside his plate.

"I'm sorry."

He shakes his head. "I'm okay. I mean, my dad was good to me, even though there were many times we didn't see eye to eye."

Nodding in understanding, I realize I have something in common with him. My parents don't understand why I don't want to work in the medical field. But it's just never been something I've been interested in. I admire them, and all medical staff, but it's not me.

"And you?" I question Brock, who's silently eating his dinner. Those blue eyes snap in my direction, meeting mine. "What about your family?"

"Four brothers, one older, two younger. My mother and father are no longer around." When he says this, my heart aches. There's a sadness in his gaze that tears at my chest. "Not really much to tell." He shrugs it off, and I can see the pain in his eyes. I don't push, allowing the subject to change when Ethan prompts me about what I plan to do after school.

"I want to work for myself. I'd like to offer clients marketing advice and help them get their business off the ground."

"Nice." He smiles, and once again, my stomach flips.

We sit in silence for a little while, eating our dinner, and I can't help taking both boys in. They're so different, so very opposite to each other. I observe them quietly as they ask each other for objects from the table—their touches, smiles, gazes. There's a connection between them.

"Are you two...?" I start, unsure of what to say, or how to ask it. "I mean, I know..." I've never been so nervous to ask something before. My family is rather close minded when it comes to certain things, certain lifestyles, which makes me sad, but I think it's amazing when people love each other without qualms.

"We're not together just yet, but we care about each other. If that's what you wanted to know." Ethan puts me out of my misery with his response.

Nodding, I smile. "Yeah, I mean...I just...there's clearly affection at the table and your home isn't what I was expecting."

"Trust me, it's not always this clean," Brock chimes in. "Normally, there are clothes on every piece of furniture." He laughs, the sound light and carefree, and for the first time since I've met him, I see a different Brock.

NINE

B R O C K

SHE LOOKS AT ME STRANGELY FOR A MOMENT. NOT in a bad way, but almost as if she's attempting to decipher me. The only person who's ever been able to do that is Ethan. Her eyes are unique, almost cat-like in shape, and they're blue, but not like mine. Hers are deep, endless, and remind me of the ocean.

"So," she starts, a soft pink on her cheeks as she blushes, and I know she's going to ask about sex. "You two always share?"

"Not always, only when the woman is exquisite." Ethan's compliment causes her cheeks to darken even more. She's fucking beautiful. Many times, over the years, I've been with girls, women, and I'd say they're hot, or fuckable, or something like that, but with Camila, she's none of those things.

She's breathtaking.

The thought stops me for a moment.

Being like my dad, I've always been the "hit it and quit it" type, but with her, I think I may just become an addict to her taste, her smile, and that incredibly sexy caramel skin. I imagine she tastes as sweet.

"I'm no prude, but I've never been with two guys," she whispers. There's no judgment, though, just pure innocence.

"Are you...?" I want to ask her if she's a virgin, to be up front, but I can't find the words.

She shakes her head. "No, I mean, I've had boyfriends." She smiles shyly, her long dark lashes fluttering against the apples of her cheeks. *Jesus, she's incredible.*

"Then we'll take it slow," Ethan confirms with a nod.

She smiles, and my heart fills with something I've only ever felt when I'm with Ethan. Strangely, it doesn't make me fear what I feel, it's almost like a certain freedom.

Perhaps that's how my dad felt when he first looked at Rowan. I certainly never felt that way about my ex-girlfriend. When Dad "stole" her from me, I wasn't really that broken up about it. I got my car he promised and he got the girl. My pride suffered a blow for about a day, but every time I revved that engine, I knew who really won.

Camila picks up her drink, swallowing the wine, glances at Ethan, then meets my eyes, blue on blue. Her lips are wet with the red liquid, and I'm tempted to lick them, suck them, and make her whimper when I bite down on the plump flesh.

My cock thickens at the sight as the thoughts tumble in my mind. *Fuck.*

I lower my eyes, focusing on my food until the plate is empty, leaving Ethan and her to talk about school and her love for surfing. I catch every nuance, every smile and glimmer as she talks about her love of the ocean.

Camila rises and takes her plate into the kitchen. When she returns, she heads to the window to watch the waves beyond.

"How about we relax in the living room for a while?" I suggest once all our plates are cleared and the wine glasses are empty.

"Sure. I can't stay out too late, though. My dad won't like it," Camila informs us.

I shove my chair back, rising and heading toward her. "Is he that strict?" I question, reminding myself of how Levi and my dad allowed us to live our lives the way we wanted. Most days, they probably didn't know where we were.

"Yeah, just a tad. I'm the youngest," she tells me.

"Ah, the baby," Ethan teases, earning him a feisty glare. I chuckle. She's fire and warmth, and I lean in to plant a kiss on her forehead. She tilts her face, and her eyes meet mine. There's desire there, beautiful and shiny. Ethan joins us, his hands holding onto her bare arms, mine on her hips. We're once again cocooning her, keeping her between us where, somewhere deep down, I know she's meant to be.

"Can I ask you something?" Her tone is breathy, making it clear she loves being sandwiched between us.

"Sure." I nod.

"Do you...can you..." she flits her gaze between us, "kiss?"

Her question stills me for a moment. That was the last thing I expected her to say. I look up at my best friend, and he shrugs. After our leap forward recently, this will be a walk in the park. I step away from Camila and toward Ethan, but out the corner of my eye, I see her full lips part on a gasp when Ethan grips my nape, tugging me closer. Rough, forceful, pure alpha male.

Our lips mesh after a moment, and I can't stop the growl he elicits. Her breath hitches beside me, and I can feel her eyes burning into us, searing me, scorching him. She likes this.

My tongue duels with Ethan's, hot and wet. My cock throbs, hardening for him—for my best friend.

Our bodies are pressed tightly together. Hard and unyielding. Needy and wanton. When I open my eyes, I meet Camila's stare filled with awe and desire.

"Are you enjoying watching us, naughty girl?" I ask her.

"Yes," she responds shyly, her cheeks turning a soft pink. Her lips part when I reach for her chin, lifting her head so her eyes are on mine.

"Are you wet, baby girl?" My question has her blush darkening, the color turning her face and neck crimson. "You are. Those panties are probably drenched for us," I taunt her, earning a smile.

"Touch your pretty panties for us, sweetheart," Ethan says, his voice low, dripping with desire. The electric current hanging around us is all consuming and I'm lost in this scene.

"Go on, baby girl," I encourage her.

She shyly moves her hand down her slim frame toward her pussy. Camila's whimper causes my cock to jolt and her delicate fingers disappear between her thighs.

"In those panties, I want to see how wet you are," I tell her.

Her caramel legs are on display, and I almost lose all control when she pulls her fingers away and they're glistening with arousal.

"Fuck, baby girl," I growl, leaning into capture her fingers in my mouth. Her taste is sweet, tangy, like salted caramel. Everything I imagined and more. Fucking delicious. Once I've cleaned her fingers, I press an open-mouthed kiss on Ethan, allowing him to taste her from me.

It's only been a few days since we met the little Spanish beauty, but there's something more going on between the three of us, and I can't wait to finally experience it. When I break the kiss, I lean closer to her, inhaling her sweet scent. Ethan mimics me, cocooning her.

I'm about to pull her between us when a cell phone rings from somewhere in the house. Camila races inside, leaving us staring at her. When she picks up her phone, she frowns at the message, then looks up at us both. "I don't want to go, but my dad is worried about me," Camila says.

"Did you want me to drive you home?" Ethan questions, concern is clear in his voice.

"It's okay. I have my car," she says, smiling, and we both venture toward her.

"Soon, we'll get to devour you, but the slower the journey, the more explosive the arrival," I promise her, because I can't wait for it. She shivers at my words, and I smirk. I want her, I want this. And we'll have it really soon.

TEN

E T H A N

"**W**ANT TO CATCH SOME WAVES?" CAMILA'S voice comes from behind me. She smiles, her hand on the board in the sand next to her—a vision under the hot sun. The sand is warm underfoot, and I can feel Brock's gaze lingering on me from behind. He's on the lounger after an hour in the ocean, taking in the scenery.

After our dinner a couple weeks ago, we haven't seen Camila outside of school. Even though we haven't had a chance to spend time alone with her again, we're constantly texting each other and we meet up with her for lunch when she's not studying. There's something different about her. She doesn't get on our nerves like most women. She's not clingy, and that makes us want to spend more time with her.

With this being our last year in college, our schedules are more intense and loaded, so we've been busy. But we're both eager to see more of her.

"Sounds good," I tell her, grabbing my board and heading toward the crashing waves. As we wade through the breakers, I glance at her, reveling in the strength as she swims up beside me on her board. She's tiny, and her board is small, which makes it harder to navigate.

Her skin shimmers in the sunlight, making her look like she's glowing, and I have to turn away again so I don't end up with a fucking hard-on. A swell starts not far from us, and her squeal is enough to tell me she's about to catch this one.

Her swift movements are intoxicating. Watching her is like watching a dolphin in its element, in the water, drenched, happy, and glowing with a smile that lights my whole fucking world. Only one other person makes me feel like this. Brock.

I join her, easily hopping onto the surface of my surfboard and riding the wave alongside her. We weave around each other, as if we're dancing on the clear blue ocean, but not the same color as my best friend's eyes— not the same color that makes me heart thud just that much faster.

We're nearing the shore as the crest slows, and I slide off. The line tugs at my ankle, bringing the board back to me.

"Should we head over to Brock and keep him company?" Camila gestures to where the man in question is now on his stomach, facing the apartment instead of the beach. I glance over at her and chuckle. Mischief twinkles in her eyes. I know exactly what she has in mind.

"Let's go." Picking up my board, I race behind her as she makes her way up to Brock. As soon as she reaches him, she shakes her long curls over him, dripping cold water all over his tan, smooth back.

"Fuck!"

Camila squeals when he's on his feet, chasing her down toward the water. They run by me, right into the wave crashing on the shore, and once again, Brock is soaked. His face lights up with happiness. When they reach me again, Camila leaps into my arms, and I'm convinced we've found our girl. She makes us both happy—she makes us feel content to just relax with her. We can hold a conversation about anything and she'll match us with her knowledge. Her independence is a turn on. Her smile makes my heart beat just that much faster, and her sassiness is something that makes me want to challenge her even more.

She always has something interesting to tell us, and enjoys telling us about her classes, new books she's reading, or even discussing her Art History assignments with as much confidence as if she we're talking about surfing. Her love of the ocean leaves me in awe.

We've learned about her family moving from Spain, and her stepsister, who's not her favorite person, but all that just makes me want to delve deeper into her mind.

In the time we've known her, Brock, nor I, have looked at another woman. We haven't even spoken about heading out to any of the clubs.

I've seen a change in him over the past couple weeks, and I hope this is going to be Brock moving forward. He's been in the dark for far too long, and it hurts me to see him like that, to see his pain.

"I think we may need to head inside," I tell them. Both nod in agreement, and I wonder if this is the moment we'll finally step into unknown territory. Not for us, but for Camila. There's still a certain innocence to her, and I want to see her unravel. But instead of letting her walk out the door and go when we're done, I want to tug her back to us and keep her.

I didn't think I'd ever be able to see a woman I care about with another man, but Brock has changed me in profound ways. My dad and Eric used to play like this. Do the same things we do. But they didn't want love. They were just getting their dicks wet, whereas Brock and I care about each other, and we care about Camila.

In the apartment, I set my board out on the patio, alongside the other two. Brock and Camila head inside, and I follow.

"Shower?" Brock suggests, and I nod, my eyes on Camila. This is it. Time for her to decide.

Her big blue eyes flit between me and my best friend, and a small smile curls her perfect lips. The answer is written all over her face, but she needs to voice it. I want to hear her say the words.

"I'd like that," she offers shyly, making my dick hard.

"Brock will lead the way," I tell her, stepping up behind her.

"Into temptation?" she quips, a soft, nervous laugh tumbling from her.

He glances back at her as he laces his fingers through hers. "Is there any other place?" He chuckles, and her cheeks darken at the insinuation.

"Not when you're between us," I whisper along her bare shoulder, causing goosebumps to rise on her skin.

We make our way farther into the apartment toward the bathroom. Brock releases Camila to turn on the two showerheads in the four-person shower. Even though we've lived here for a while, we've never used it like this. Each time we've been with a girl, we've had her in our bedrooms or on the sofa.

But this is different. I care about the girl. I want to make her happy, to see her smile, and show her pleasure. And when Brock glances at me, I know he does too.

He pulls her under the spray, and I follow. The heat of the water and the heat between the three of us seems to simmer like a pot about to boil over. And nothing we do now can stop it. This was going to happen, regardless of when and where.

I tug at the string on her bikini top, allowing the material to fall free, and for the first time since I looked at her, I no longer have any doubt. Her breasts are a small handful, perfect, pert. Her nipples are dark brown, and they pebble at the heated gaze Brock offers her.

I crouch down behind her, tugging the bikini bottoms from her hips down her toned legs. Her body is utter perfection. Smooth, caramel skin. Her ass is grabbable, and I find my hands on the cheeks immediately.

"Open your legs, baby girl," Brock coos, and she obeys. Finding her core, I lean in and flick my tongue over her opening, all the way up to the small tight hole my cock aches to slide into.

Brock's mouth is on her tits, lapping and suckling while I devour her body. Her delicate hands work his shorts, and soon, they're pooled at his feet. She fists his shaft, stroking back and forth, up and down.

The sounds of desire filter down to me, and Camila glances over her shoulder at me.

"Please," she mumbles. "Kiss me."

I rise easily, wanting nothing more than to give her everything she needs and wants. Her arousal is on my tongue, on my lips, and I crash my mouth onto hers.

The gentle way her lips mold to mine makes me want to consume her even more. To take her right here, between my body and Brock's. I want to feel her shudder and tremble when we both slide into her. The way her hands slide over my shoulders, holding onto me, makes me feel stronger, more in control than I ever have.

Brock's hands on her hips hold her steady. We don't move for a moment. His cock must be aching the same way mine is. She pulls back, her eyes shimmering with need.

"You're a bad girl," I groan when her hips roll, pressing her core against my shaft. She whimpers in response when Brock's lips find her neck, suckling on the flesh.

"You taste so sweet, darling," he mumbles over her skin.

ELEVEN ——————

C A M I L A

I CAN'T DESCRIBE IT.

There are no words I can offer. This is different.

Ethan leans in to kiss Brock, and my body clenches with want and need. Watching them touch, their tongues fighting and dancing so sensually, makes my core pulse. I've always loved seeing people in love, and there's no doubt they are completely obsessed with each other.

"That's so hot," I utter, causing them to turn to me. Even though they'd just been kissing, their hands never strayed from me. Threesomes always made me wonder if the third person felt left out, like sitting on the sidelines, but they haven't made me feel like that.

Ethan pulls me even closer, his body hard behind mine. Brock's hands are on my breasts, his blue eyes electric as takes in every inch of me. His mouth latches onto my nipple, tugging and suckling, causing my clit to throb. As if Ethan can read my mind, his fingers find my pussy, circling the hard nub, pressing down on it, making me whimper. His lips trail along my neck, sucking the flesh, biting down hard.

He's marking me, and I can't stop him. I'm putty in the hands of two sculptors and there's nowhere else I'd rather be. We have a connection, something more than just a quick fuck, and the way they treat me, like a princess, it seems they've seen it too.

"We're safe," Brock starts, looking deep into my eyes. "Please tell me you're on the pill." It's a plea. He wants this as much as I do—as much as Ethan does.

"I am." My affirmation is all the boys are waiting for. Brock nods, his crooked smile giving me a glimpse of the naughty devil beneath the handsome man.

Ethan slips two fingers into my heat, plunging in and pulling out, slow and gentle, and my knees almost buckle under the weight of pleasure. Brock's mouth travels over my breasts, down my stomach, and when he reaches my pussy, he teases my clit as Ethan finger fucks me into oblivion.

My cries are otherworldly. I'm begging. I'm pleading. I'm coming hard. My legs tremble and shake. My body is merely a puppet on a string.

"So fucking beautiful," Ethan coos in my ear, sending ripples of want through me. As he tugs his fingers from me, he brings them up to my mouth. "Taste your sweet juices, sweetheart," he orders in a low, commanding tone. "Do you like making a mess on my fingers?"

I can't find my voice, so I merely nod. Brock rises, his eyes burning into me as he watches me suck my arousal from his best friend's fingers. There's a raw desire flashing in his gaze, and I don't have to look at Ethan to know there is.

A second later, I'm lifted by Brock, my legs wrapping around him easily. His hard cock nudges my entrance.

And without warning, I'm impaled on his thickness, causing another cry to be ripped from my throat. I can't think straight as Ethan starts teasing my ass, his fingers probing the tight ring of muscle.

"Trust me, sweetheart?" I nod to Ethan. I can't speak anymore. And then I feel the pressure. One finger pushes its way into me, which causes Brock to growl as I squeeze him harder at the intrusion.

"You feel far too good, baby girl." The man with the sharp blue stare grunts as he plunges into me, again and again. Another finger works its way into me, and I'm lost in delirium. Ethan works my hole, opening me, and I'm soon boneless between the two hottest men I've ever met.

Something cool and slippery accompanies a second finger that easily slips into me as he scissors me open. He continues to tease my pussy, and I relax against Brock who's holding onto me.

More cool liquid is drenched around my back

entrance, then he moves quickly, because as soon as his fingers are gone, something much larger, and harder, nudges me. The searing pain that accompanies the tip of his cock causes me to screech loudly as sharp pleasure zips through me like an electric shock.

They both still as an erotic symphony of our heavy breathing and the cascading water surrounds us.

"Move. Please...do something," I plead, finding it in me to finally ask for more.

Ethan and Brock move in sync, fingers on my clit, a mouth on my nipple, and two thick, hard cocks sliding into me. I'm sandwiched. I'm warm and cared for, and I'm about to leap over the edge into a heavenly abyss of pleasure.

The deep growls and heavy grunts from both men vibrate through me. Ethan pinches my clit hard, and I scream out my orgasm. My toes curl, my throat burns, and the sounds that fall from my lips are feral. I don't recognize myself.

Seconds later, I feel warmth as they both empty themselves inside me, and I know I'll never be the same again.

TWELVE ———

B R O C K

As soon as I pull into the parking lot, I'm out of the car and grabbing the bags of ice we needed for the party. Even though the apartment is fully stocked, we always run out. By the time I reach the top floor, the music is booming and there are scantily clad women all over the living room.

A few guys from school are already making moves on the ladies, and the party is in full swing. The kitchen is the quietest room in the whole place, where I find Ethan and Camila. She's dressed in a bright yellow bikini that cups a pair of small tits I'm dying to bite and mark.

"Hey, baby girl." I offer her a wink as I set the bags on the counter.

"Hi, Brock." She smiles, and I find myself hungry for

more of them. Her face lights up, and mischief twinkles in her eyes. She may play the innocent card, but there's a little tigress hidden beneath that shy exterior.

When I meet my best friend's gaze, he looks worried. "What?" I ask.

He sighs, raking his fingers through his unruly dark hair. He must've been in the pool because it's even darker than normal and dripping onto his bare shoulders.

"Your brother is here," he tells me.

"Already?" I ask, confused.

"Yeah. He got an Uber," Ethan chuckles.

I groan. *Fuck.* I forgot to pick him up at the airport, but my clever ass brother found me. Hayden will kill me if he knew I dropped the ball on this. Luckily, Camden would never rat me out.

"Okay," I respond in a long sigh. "I hope he's not drinking. He's far too young." I shove the last bag of ice into the freezer before turning to Ethan.

"No, he's behaving. Sort of," he grumbles.

"What do you mean sort of?" As soon as the question leaves my lips, I'm met with a series of giggles from the doorway. When I turn, I find my youngest brother with two college girls on either arm. They're dressed in next to nothing, their nipples peeking out and on show through their white bikinis.

"Brock!" He offers me a happy, wide smile, knocking the breath from my lungs. He looks so much like our dad, it's uncanny. We all do, but it's the fact that he's got these bimbos draped over him like he's the goddamn playboy king.

"Get the fuck off my brother," I bite out, shoving both women into the living room and dragging Camden into the kitchen. "I'm sorry I forg—"

"Don't stress, Brock. I'm a grown ass man." He winks confidently. "I don't need a babysitter." His features darken and his jaw clenches. Sometimes, behind his playful smiles, something lurks. And after all we went through with Nixon and his crazy ass, I worry about

Camden.

Guilt still surges through me at forgetting him at the airport. I'm such a dick. I promised myself I'd never turn into Dad. *Fuck this.* Pulling him into my arms, I give my little brother—who's every bit as big and filled out as me—a hug, squeezing him.

"I've missed you," I tell him, feeling tears sting my eyes. I blink them away, swallowing past the emotion. When I step back, I take in the boy I watched grow up who's now a man. I can't deny he's going to break some hearts, if he hasn't already. "And stop working out so much. You may get bigger than me one day, but I'll always be able to kick your ass."

"You keep telling yourself that." Camden smirks. "I wanted to see what sort of trouble you're getting yourself into here on the West Coast." He grins wickedly at me.

"And you're certain you came here because of brotherly love?" I tease him, gesturing to the two girls who are still eye-fucking my brother.

"Well, I can't not appreciate your view." He shrugs, and then his gaze grows stormy. "I deserve a break after nailing that debate competition."

"Your debate team won?"

"Of course we did," he says smugly.

"I figured. Just don't drink, and don't do anything I wouldn't do," I tell him, feeling Camila's stare burning a hole right through me. I wonder if she's intrigued by this side of me only Ethan sees.

When my brother disappears into the crowd, I turn to Ethan and Camila.

"I can see the family resemblance," she says with a fond smile.

Shaking my head, I grab a beer from the ice bucket and face her. "Everyone says that. We take after our father."

"Is that a good thing or a bad thing?" she smiles sweetly, and I'm once again knocked breathless by her beauty.

"Depends who's asking," I shrug.

"Being that I was an only child for a long time, I found being with the Pearsons has given me an idea of what it's like with siblings, and as much as I don't think I could've enjoyed having younger brothers, I have to be the big brother now," Ethan chuckles. When Camila pins him with a questioning gaze, he explains. "My dad remarried and I now have a little sister."

"And how do you feel about it?" Her question stills us both. Not because Ethan isn't happy, but because there was tension between him and his dad for years.

"I'm happy for him." His gaze meets mine, honesty shining through, and I smile. "He's found someone to love, he has a daughter, and I have my family here." My best friend glances my way.

"I like that you were able to find something real." Camila smiles, looking at us both as she sips her drink. "To be honest, I was scared...well..." she mulls over her words, tipping her head to the side, "nervous, but I've never been more at ease with two people. Ever."

I nod, settling in beside her. I want to touch her, but I don't—not yet. Even though we have already been inside her, touching her, fucking her, this conversation needed to happen. We need to make her see this was never just for fun, because I care for her, and Ethan does too.

"And that's the beauty about having a connection. Listen to me, Camila, you're not some one-night stand to us. You're—"

"So much more," Ethan finishes.

"What?" she gasps, those big blue eyes flitting between me and him.

"You know our rather unique tastes," I tell her, trailing my fingertips over the curve of her shoulder, reveling in the goosebumps that rise in the wake of my touch. "And we wanted to talk this over with you."

She swallows. "Like, a relationship?" she murmurs in shock. It's new to us as well. There's never been a woman I wanted something long-term with.

"Yes." Ethan's voice is cool, calm, and as always, deep and rumbling.

"Wow." Her voice is filled with shock. "I've never thought about it."

"You're not scared?" My question causes her head to tip my way. Silence hangs between us, and when I'm certain she'll refuse, she shrugs.

"No. It's not that," she starts, lowering her gaze as she decides how to tell us what's bothering her. "I've just...I mean, you know I told you my father is strict, he's—"

"Don't worry about that right this moment," I respond. "We need to talk about how you feel about this. If you're willing to try, we can always win over your father's approval. Trust me," I wink cockily, "Ethan's great at being the good guy." I swipe the bottle and leave Ethan to the girl who's stolen both our hearts.

THIRTEEN ——————

E T H A N

THE MOON IS HIGH IN THE DARK SKY. I SIP MY BEER AS I stare out at the water, listening to the stragglers say goodnight to Brock who's shutting the door behind them. The only person left is Camila. After our chat, she made her way outside, and I left her to mull over our proposal. She's lazing at the pool, her feet in the water. I want to go to her, but instead, I revel in watching her swirl her feet in the lit-up pool.

"Do you think she'll say yes?" Brock questions from beside me.

Nodding, I respond. "She will. I mean, she wanted this with us. I don't think her nervousness is about being between us anymore, it's about her family."

Brock nods, and we both take a moment to watch

her. There's a sensuality she exudes, even in the way she tips her head back, looking up at the sky. It's intoxicating to watch.

"Where's Cam? Still enjoying the *view* with those two chicks?" I glance over at Brock.

"Nah, he's in the guestroom working on some *research* he didn't want to talk about. It's as if he's older than me at times." This time, he chuckles. It's almost two in the morning and I'm tired. The only thing keeping me going is Camila.

We head toward the swimming pool, like two hungry lions about to devour Bambi. She turns her head on our approach and smiles.

"You're not tired?" I ask, settling beside her on the concrete edge. My legs dip into the water, then I push off and emerge myself up to my chest in the pool.

She smiles, shaking her head. "Not really. I normally stay up late when I'm working on a project, or just reading." There's a gentleness to her, and I watch as

Brock takes her hand in his.

"You survived your first Pearson and Kingston party," he offers with a wolfish smirk, pressing a kiss to her knuckles. "Figured it would've worn you out, but we'd gladly wear you out in another way."

A soft laugh falls from her glossy lips. "It really wasn't as bad as you made it out to be. And I think we should take a raincheck on the after party. Your brother is here," she says. Her confidence makes me smile.

My best friend nods, and I wade closer to her, moving between her legs. "There are times the parties get a little out of hand." Placing my hands on her thighs, I stroke her smooth skin, reaching the edge of her bikini bottoms, and a dick-hardening whimper falls from her plump lips.

"Shhh, sweetheart. Just let it be." My fingers gently urge her body on, causing a tremble to race through her. There's one thing I've learned about Camila—she's exquisite when she unravels. But that's not what I want right now. Tonight, I'll tease and taunt her, and leave her needy. Anticipation is all about the push and pull.

"Ethan," she murmurs.

"Tell us you want this as much as we do?" Brock coaxes her as he suckles the smooth skin on the nape of her neck. His lips trail gently over her, making her shiver, and I watch as goosebumps rise up over her flesh. Under my fingers, she feels warm, and I know her body is ready to take us again.

"I like you." Her eyes are on him, then on me. "And I like you too." Her confession stirs something in my gut, ensuring my cock is now tenting my shorts. I push her thighs wider. The material covering her pussy is tight against the lips. Pressing a thumb to her mound, I stroke up, then down along the slit, making her hips buck against me.

We need to take it slow, because I feel like I'm falling for her. How can I want both of them? Isn't that being selfish? There are people out there who only ever find one soul mate, one person that completes them, how is it I've found two?

I lift my eyes toward Brock, telling him with one look what I think, and he nods. We've done this plenty of times before, but Camila is so different. I want our time together to be special. Her head drops back and she closes her eyes as I lean in and plant a soft kiss on her pussy. Another soft mewl tumbles through the dark night, hanging between the three of us as my best friend captures her nipple in his mouth over the material of her bathing suit. He goes to work, teasing it, and he reaches for her other tit, groping and fondling. Her hips roll, trying to get closer to my face. We continue our assault on her body until she's whimpering and shuddering. Our hands are on her, steadying her as she rides out the pleasure. When she finally looks at me again, her gaze is shimmering with need.

Not tonight, sweetheart.

"Are you ready? Brock will drop you off at home," I tell her.

She flits her gaze between us, suddenly unsure of why we're sending her home. The thing is, if she stays any longer, I'm going to rip these damn bikini bottoms from her pretty little hips and eat her pussy until she's screaming so loud, all of goddamn L.A. will hear her.

"We'll see you tomorrow," Brock smiles, settling her confusion. "Tonight, we want you to think about what we said. If you're willing to try this, a relationship between the three of us—"

"It will be something that's new to all of us. But if you stay here, we'll just distract you and make you agree." I wink at her, causing her to giggle. The sound is beautiful and melodic, and I want to hear it again. I want to listen to it on repeat. Forever.

"Dinner is on us tomorrow," Brock informs her with a cocky smirk.

"You mean I'm cooking and you're drinking?" I arch an eyebrow at him, eliciting another laugh from Camila. "There is no pressure to say yes. If all you want is short-term," I squeeze her thighs, "then that's what we'll offer you."

"I get it. I'll have an answer for you tomorrow. I promise." The look in her eyes tells me she's already got an answer. And I'm certain it's *yes*. But time will tell.

"Good girl." I smile. "Brock will drive you home. I've had one too many beers." We've learned the hard way that our parties tend to get wild, so one of us is normally the designated adult, and tonight, it's Brock's turn.

FOURTEEN

BROCK

"**O**KAY," SHE ANSWERS, AND I GRIN.

"Good," I rise, offering her my hand. Ethan is out of the pool, rounding us. She's pinned between us, held hostage by our bodies. I lift her chin, forcing her to look into my eyes. "And tomorrow, all bets are off," I inform her. "Tomorrow, I want to make your pretty little body tremble until you're passed out from all the pleasure we'll bestow on you." My promise makes her shiver.

"I can't wait to lick you, taste you, devour you, Camila," Ethan whispers in her ear, moving her curls from her neck. He suckles on the sweet, caramel flesh, licking and tasting her. Watching them makes me harder than rock.

"Ethan," she whimpers, dropping her head to the

side, offering him better access, as if he's a vampire about to devour her. *Fuck.* I'm solid steel, making my swim shorts rather uncomfortable.

"Let's go," I announce, stepping away from her heat.

Moments later, we're in the car, and she gives me her address. For some reason, seeing her working at the shack, I thought perhaps she needed the money, but when I pull up to the mansion that reminds me of my childhood home, I'm shocked at the size.

"This is me," she tells me with a shy smile.

"Don't put on that act," I tell her. "Shy girls only get so far." My eyes land on hers. "Just beneath that shy exterior is a little vixen wanting to be freed."

"You caught me," she laughs, a beautiful, melodic sound that comes straight from her gut.

"Tomorrow." I lean in, my lips whispering over her cheek. "We'll have some fun."

She nods, exiting the car. I wait until I see her disappear behind the high gates. I wonder why the fuck she'd be working when she's as rich as Ethan and I. Shaking my head, I pull back onto the road and make my way home.

Moments later, I'm walking into the living room, my mind still on Camila. Ethan is lounging on the couch with the TV on, the volume so low, there's not even a hum in the background, a pair of gray sweatpants hanging low on his hips. He's toned and tan, chiseled with a dark trail of hair that runs from beneath his belly button to his thick cock.

Everything about him oozes sex. From the smirk that curls his full lips to the way he grips the beer bottle in his hand. His fingers can make a woman scream his name, his mouth can have her finding religion, but it's his eyes that don't hide what he's really feeling—they hold mischief and pain.

We connected on that pain. It was what brought us together, and throughout the years, it became more than that. I don't think my brothers understand me. I didn't think anyone would, and then he came along and showed me there is life after death. No matter the circumstances of that death, those who live on will continue their journey through life's ups and downs.

"Hey." I settle on the sofa beside him. Grabbing his beer, I put it to my lips and take a long swig. The bubbles fizzle down my throat as I swallow the alcohol. He doesn't respond, merely watches me as I set the beer down on the coffee table.

He reaches for me, his hand behind my head, and pulls me toward him. Our lips crash against each other like a storm rolling in. Thunder strikes when our tongues tangle, and I'm ready to take this into the bedroom, or wherever we can continue. Since we first kissed and then sucked each other off, it knocked me on my ass. I knew it would be different with him, but what I felt, what my body needed, was so much more.

All my life I knew I was different, that I didn't just want women, but it was only when I spent more time with Ethan did I realize it was him. It was always him. I don't doubt for a moment that when we finally took this step, there'd be no way of coming back from it. And I know he feels the same.

When he finally pulls away, his dark eyes shine with emotion.

"What's wrong?" I question. He's been quiet today, and it slowly dawns on me what today is. *Shit.* I totally forgot. "Shit, I'm sorry." I scrub my hand over my jaw.

"It's fine," he tells me, but it's not. "I just needed..." A sigh. One that grips my chest. As much as he saved me, I realize now just how much I mean to him.

"Hey," I say, grabbing his thigh and pulling it closer to me. "I know it never gets easier."

He nods, but doesn't respond. We sit in silence for a while, staring out the window, listening to the waves crashing on the shore. I recall my own mother. As much as I loved my dad, she was just as bad as he was when it came to fucking around.

"Mom?" I call out, wondering if she's home. Nixon and Camden aren't back yet, and I wander through the house, knowing Hayden is probably out with his friends.

"What the fuck?" I hear my father's deep rumble. I know he's been with other women. I saw him in town, not hiding the fact that he had his hand on some skinny blonde's butt. Shuddering at the memory, I creep closer to their bedroom.

"You've been doing it for years, Eric," Mom hisses angrily. Her hand flies up, slapping my dad on his cheek. He looks like he's been out all night. His shirt, normally ironed to perfection, is rumpled and he looks like hell.

"Fuck you, okay! You don't give me what I need," Dad bites back, tugging his shirt free. When it falls to the floor, I notice the scratches on his back and wonder who hurt him. Maybe it was the blonde woman, or maybe another woman I didn't see him with.

"Oh? Like what? You wanted kids. You wanted this fucking house, now I'm left here to fend for myself."

"That's bullshit, and you know it. My boys need a parent while I'm at work. Why don't you act like a mother and care for them?" Another harsh slap that echoes through the small space.

"I am a good mother," she utters, but it's a lie. My mother hasn't been there for us in years. My eyes fill with angry tears when she mumbles, *"I love my boys, but you, Eric Pearson... you're a fucking cheating asshole."*

I turn away, not wanting to know more about the pain in our home. From the outside, it's beautiful, pristine, but the ugliness within these walls makes me sick.

I hate the lies.

All of them.

I just want to run away and never come back.

And something tells me, if I did, they wouldn't even miss me. Not Hayden, not Nixon, and not my parents. The only thing that stops me from leaving is my little brother, Camden.

FIFTEEN ——————

E T H A N

"YOU'RE LOST INSIDE YOUR HEAD AGAIN," I TELL him, snapping him out of whatever memory had hold of him. Today was the anniversary of my mother's death. I tried to push the sadness into the back of my mind, and when the apartment was filled with people I didn't really know, I could focus on anything but that—but her. However, as soon as I was alone, it slammed into me, reminding me she's no longer here.

Even though it's been years, there's still an ache that seems to linger. It's as if she's reminding me she loves me.

Unlike Brock's mother, mine was loving and spent all her time with me. She was there for me during the moments I learned what I loved—my love of art, surfing—and she gave me the love my father couldn't offer once she was gone. When she died, I was angry. I blamed my dad for her leaving us, even though I knew it wasn't his fault. She was ill. Seeing her wither away was more painful than her dying because she was so strong, and as she grew weaker, it hurt me more than I could've imagined. It took me years to realize my father hurt as well.

He just showed it in a different way. He fell into a life of women and work. Even though he provided for me, buying me anything I needed, he couldn't deal with a wayward teenager who believed he knew everything.

"I'm sorry I forgot," Brock tells me, turning to face me. The heat of his hand on my thigh isn't helping clear my head. Between the sadness of today, and the way my body reacts to him, I'm a tornado of emotion.

"You don't need to apologize," I tell him. Meeting those blue eyes, I feel them search my soul. We took a step into the unknown not so long ago—something that's always been there, but we never acted on. Now, though, I no longer want to hide my feelings for him. I know I love him, more than a friend, more than I ever thought possible. Our friendship started easily, but it was when I realized my feelings ran much deeper that I finally admitted to myself I was different.

Brock turns his attention my way. "There are so many reasons I don't feel like going back home," he finally admits what I know has been bothering him. "But I know I need to."

"You do," I tell him. Leaning forward, I grip the back of his head, pulling him in for another heated kiss. Our lips touch for a moment. This is new territory for us, just being together. We leaped over the edge, we freed ourselves of the hidden feelings we've kept at bay for so long. There's only so much a barrier can take before it shatters and torrents break free.

I've wanted him.

Needed him, but this...I wasn't prepared for it.

There's so much more in this kiss.

His tongue delves into my mouth, tasting the bitter alcohol. We fight for dominance, neither giving up to the other. His hard body is against mine in seconds. My cock throbs as he hovers over me. I grind my hips up against him, and he follows suit.

Dry humping my best friend, I can't tamper the groan that rumbles in my chest at the friction his thigh offers my cock. Two strong, chiseled bodies smashed together with a flurry of need. His hand grips my dick, and mine returns the favor.

Rough. Fast. Unrestrained.

We move together, kissing, panting like hungry animals. He grips me as roughly as I do him, and I feel it. My balls tighten, drawing up, needing to find release. As I grunt mine out into my boxer briefs, I feel warmth against my hand.

There aren't any sounds in the living room. No music. No talking. Just us. Breathing. Heat burns in Brock's gaze, and I know I'm offering him the same look back. It's done. We're something more now, and there's no longer any denying it.

"Well," he murmurs, looking at me, turned on and utterly immersed in the desire swimming in his clear blue eyes.

"I guess that took care of that," I tell him, the corner of my mouth kicking into a full-on grin.

"We need to talk about that." He moves off me, a wet spot visible in his shorts. "There's no way we can still just be friends."

"We never were *just* friends. You said so yourself," I tell him. Shrugging, I swig my beer, downing the whole bottle in one long swallow, trying to stay calm. When I meet his eyes, I notice it—a wolfish grin curling his lips.

"We're official then?"

"I guess we are, asshole," I chuckle, placing the bottle on the table.

"Then we'll have to tell Camila what she's getting herself into," he says, smirking, eyes shining with mischief.

"Do you think she'll mind? I don't. We can't deny this anymore."

"Yeah, we're past the pretenses now." He nods, rising from the sofa. "I have to tell my family, my brothers. I can't live in denial. Not that I was," he adds quickly. "I just mean...for so long, I've tried to tell myself nothing was going on between us."

"I know. My father knows," I tell him. Levi isn't stupid. He's known for a long while.

"Hayden and Nix definitely know, even though I haven't told them anything yet."

"I figured we'd be a one-time thing," I shrug, sitting forward, my elbows resting on my knees.

He rises, heading toward the hallway leading to the bedrooms. "Do I look like a manwhore?" He chuckles. "I won't just fuck my best friend and never do it again, you should know that by now. And besides," he stops at the entrance of the long hallway, "you know we were never going to be a one-time thing." With that, he leaves me alone in the living room with my thoughts.

SIXTEEN

C A M I L A

TWO GUYS. YOUNG, HANDSOME, AND FAR TOO RICH for their own good. As much as I should run and hide, they intrigue me. After meeting them both and spending some time with them, as friends, and then as lovers, I couldn't think of anything else.

Since they spoke to me that day, things have been intense, but I wouldn't change it. It burns brighter and hotter each day. Brock and Ethan are so different, but also, so very much alike. I don't know what they've seen in me, but their offer of a real relationship is something I thought about before they even mentioned it.

It's not normal. But then again, I've never been normal. Being unique, being different, it makes sense. My father may never accept my choice to be with them, but

I'm old enough to make my own decisions.

My stomach somersaults wildly at the thought of giving them their answer tonight. I know they're nervous. I can see it dancing in their eyes when they look at me. It's strange having so much power over two men, but I love it.

Learning about them both has given me little more insight into the two. Talking and learning about their families, I noticed the tension that races through Brock at the mention of his siblings, which makes me think they don't know about his relationship with Ethan yet.

I pull on the skirt I chose for tonight, noticing how it hugs my hips, ass, and thighs. It stops mid-thigh, and the soft blue matches my eyes. The top I'm wearing which is the color of night, with buttons down the front, is loose fitting, but offers a hint of cleavage. Not that I have much. And I can't help wondering if Brock would rip it open. Ethan is gentler when he touches and kisses me, whereas Brock is rough around the edges and his grip is feral.

They make the perfect match, and being between them is like flying. The soft and hard, the rough and gentle, and the pleasure they gave me is something I never thought possible.

"Mila." My name sounds from behind me, and I spin around. My stepsister takes me in, her dark brow arched in question. "And this?" she bites out, waving her hand up and down, referring to my outfit.

"What?" My indignant tone sets her into motion.

She stalks closer, tugging at my wild curls. "Who is he, Mila?" Her voice is a low hiss in my ear. My sister is only two years older than me, and sometimes, it feels as if she's attempting to take my mother's place in my life. However, because she's not my blood relation, she'll never be welcomed into the family. My grandmama, has already said she's no child of the Alvaro bloodline.

"*He* is none of your business, Manuela," I bite out, tugging away from her grasp. My blood simmers, awaiting her attack. The frustration of being held down, watched like a hawk, is something I always experience around her. If she would live her life and ignore me, I'd be happy. Only, it won't happen. Not when she's hated by my family.

I wish I could move out. To be far away from her would be my ultimate goal. My father would miss me, but it's time for me to find a place of my own. Or... Perhaps I could ask Brock and Ethan if I can crash in their guest room. I wonder if it's something they'd consider. If I wasn't so scared to ask, I'd do it tomorrow.

It may sound strange, but there's something between us, all three of us, and I can't forget how they both feel. Near me. Touching me. Kissing me.

"Don't you go whoring yourself out, little sister," Manuela sneers, her eyes traveling from my head to toes and back again. Then, thankfully, she spins on her heel and leaves me to get ready. Even her sour mood doesn't dampen mine. Excitement skitters over me, and I'm ready to meet the two boys who've intrigued me.

Hopefully, when I say yes, they'll give me the release my body aches for.

In more ways than one.

———

"There she is," a deep voice comes from behind me. I've been staring out at the waves for long moments, deciding on how to tell them. I turn to face both men.

"Hi." I sound far too shy. Even though I've already allowed them inside me, in more ways than one, I still feel like the innocent little girl. They make me feel good, different.

"Did you want to have dinner on the beach, or at our place?" Ethan questions, stepping up to me, planting his full lips on my forehead. It's an intimate gesture, something that tells me this is more to them.

Brock kisses my cheek, and as if they know I need comfort, they cocoon me in their warmth. For the first time since meeting them, I'm no longer nervous for what our future holds. I revel in it.

"Maybe we should go back to your place," I tell them. "We need to talk. I would like to clear up what's happening between us."

Both men look at me, and I can see the fear in their eyes, perhaps apprehension, that I'm going to walk away. It makes my heart thunder in my chest to feel so wanted and adored. I lace my fingers through Brock's, then Ethan's, and lead the way back toward their apartment. The silence between us is palpable. There's tension rolling from them in waves.

A small smile plays on my lips and I can't stop the excitement from bubbling in my stomach. I like them, and perhaps I can love them. It's too soon to even think that, but I know in my heart it wouldn't be a challenge to fall for them both.

We reach the building, and Brock shoves open the entrance door. Soon, we're inside the apartment, and I'm in the living room. I slip off my shoes, pressing my toes into the shaggy carpet. They're both standing on the other side of the sofa as if the piece of furniture is going to stop them from ravaging me.

"Is your brother still here?" I question Brock, who shakes his head.

"He headed out with some people he met at the party last night to get pizza and grab a movie. He'll be back later."

I nod. That's when I turn my back to them, and slowly unbutton the shirt I'm wearing, then slip each of the sleeves of my top from my shoulders. The cool silky material falls to the floor, and I'm standing in my skirt and a pastel blue bra.

I reach for the zipper of my skirt and pull it down, the loud hiss the only sound in the room. Shoving the material over my hips, I step out of it. As soon as I'm done, I turn to offer them the view of my front. The bra and panties I'm wearing are sheer. I've shaved completely between my legs, and my nipples are already hard under their intense scrutiny.

"Fuck." The grunt is Brock's. But there's a growl from Ethan, and there's a fire in his eyes that blazes over me from head to toe. Had I thought of him as the gentle one earlier?

"We need to take this to the bedroom," Ethan offers. Reaching for me, he tugs me closer and leads me toward the hallway. When I glance behind me, I notice Brock picking up my clothes and following close behind.

I didn't tell them my answer. I only offered them my body.

But as soon as we're in the bedroom, I'll finally voice my words.

SEVENTEEN

ETHAN

I CAN'T FATHOM WHY SHE'S AGREEING TO BE HERE. Yes, we've been amazing together, but I've always had a problem with love, with affection. It's been a long time coming, though. Brock broke through my walls and now Camila seems to have shattered the remaining bricks.

We enter my bedroom in nervous silence. My stomach is twisted in knots at the thought of her saying no. I release her hand, watching as she settles on the edge of my large, king-size bed.

The door clicks shut, and the three of us glance at each other. This is as new to us as it is Camila, and I don't blame her for being scared. Or nervous. But I just don't want her to refuse our offer. The fact that we don't just

137

want her—we need her.

"I've thought about what you said," she finally speaks in a low, confident tone. "And as much as I should say no..." She rises, reaches behind her back, and unclasps her bra.

I hold my breath, having no idea how this is going to go.

"I am saying yes." She smiles, allowing the skimpy material to fall to my black carpet. Her tits are perfect, and my tongue darts out to wet my lips, ready to devour the little kitten who seems to be in a playful mood tonight.

"Are you trying to kill us?" I quip, stalking toward her.

A small squeal tumbles free, and I'm on the bed, tugging her against me, while my best friend sheds his t-shirt and jeans. The mattress dips when he kneels behind her, my lips already latched onto her nipple, tugging and sucking it into my warm mouth.

Brock makes quick work of her panties, and soon, she's naked. I trail my fingertips over her skin, enjoying how affected she is by this simple touch.

"I wanted you to see me, to know I'm giving this everything," she tells me, then looks over at Brock. "I want you both, but I'm nervous." Her confession stills him for a moment, and he cups her face in his hands, pulling her closer. I watch as his lips feather along hers. I always thought I'd be a jealous person, watching my best friend with a woman I want, but having her want us both, enjoying both of our attention, it's euphoric.

When she looks back at me, I plant a kiss on her lips, then quietly whisper, "This isn't a game. This isn't going to end." I'm not only vowing this to her, I'm telling my best friend as well. A smile on his face, then hers, tells me they understand.

Desire hangs heavy in the room. Camila straddles me, leaning forward, and I feel my shorts get tugged down along with my boxers. My erection is right at her entrance. Her pussy is warm, and her arousal slicking my shaft is more than I can handle. I have to breathe through not losing my control and sliding into her too quickly.

She whimpers when Brock's hands open her. His tongue laps along my cock—which feels really fucking amazing—up to her pussy, and then teases her ass. The pleasure on her face shows how lost in her need for this she is. A sweet girl who was far from innocent when we took her and offered her everything she needed.

"Is this what my dirty girl wants?" Brock grits out, his fingers gently pushing into her.

Her plump lips fall open on a gasp as her nails dig into my chest.

"Ride it, baby girl," Brock coos as his free hand fists my shaft, holding me in place and guiding Camila's tight little pussy over the tip. She sinks onto me, drawing a deep pleasured groan from my chest. Her walls pulse around me when I'm fully seated inside her.

"Oh god," she moans as he continues his ministrations. I'm so fucking close to losing every ounce of restraint. I grip her hips, holding her still. Each time she rolls her body, I'm closer to filling her with my cum.

She's tight. So fucking tight.

"Please," she pleads with me, and I know the moment she loses control, I'm going to empty myself inside her.

Brock shifts, straddling my legs. I stare into Camila's blue eyes, watching her expression as he enters her. It's slow, intense, and her face only changes infinitesimally as he moves closer. As soon as he's inside, I feel his cock through the thin barrier of her body.

"Jesus, Brock." The words are a deep growl when he reaches back and grips my balls, holding me firmly as he pulls out and slowly slides back in. The feel of him is incredible. Our bodies move slowly, easing her into a position where she's spread for us both.

Her hard nipples on my chest make me groan, her whimpers are music to my ears, and the deep grunt of the man behind her is all I need to lose all sense of reality. Her right hand laces with mine, and my left hand laces with Brock's. Connected. So fucking intense, I can't hold back.

"Fuck," I bite out. The sound is basal, feral, and animalistic.

"Oh, Brock, Ethan," Camila shouts in pleasure, and I hope to god Camden isn't back as her body flutters her release. I can't hold on. My grip on her hips is vice-like, and my hips lift, pumping into her, fucking her like a crazed animal.

Brock moves faster, his cock sliding against mine inside her. He's close. We move in sync, claiming this girl, owning every inch of her.

"Fuck yes," Brock growls, and my body responds. Jet after jet of hot release fills Camila, her pussy and ass marked by us both.

EIGHTEEN

BROCK

I CAN'T HELP GROANING IN PLEASURE WHEN I FEEL bodies moving around me. Heat sears me when I feel my cock being fisted by smooth skin. My gaze snaps open and I find a pair of dark brown and a pair of blue eyes peeking up at me. Camila's smile is innocent, yet filthy at the same time. How one woman can look both like an angel and the devil is beyond me.

Ethan's hand is between her thighs, but his lips glide along my shaft along with hers. They're both sucking me into a frenzy I don't think I can hold back from. Cami's delicate hand cups my sac, holding my balls as she massages them gently.

"Fuck," I grunt, my hips lifting as I fuck my dick into Ethan's mouth. A soft giggle comes from the pretty girl with the wild hair. She moves her body so her pussy is now near my face, and I take full advantage. While my best friend and my girlfriend enjoy my body, I taunt and tease her slick little hole.

My fingers move up and down in a steady rhythm, the same one they're using on my dick. I'm not sure who's mouth is where, but I'm beyond reason.

My hips lift and my back arches as I devour the pretty little pussy now straddling my face. Her whimpers and mewls are fuel, and I continue eating her. She's sweet, musky, and so fucking silky, I can imagine my dick deep inside her body.

"Oh fuck," she cries out, then the sound is muffled. Seconds later, Ethan is on the end of the bed with a pillow on his lap, and Camila is covering her naked body with the black sheet from Ethan's bed. When I open my eyes, I find Camden leaning against the doorjamb, his arms folded in front of his chest with a smirk on his face.

"Who needs an alarm clock when you have this?" he

chortles, a devilish grin on his face as he gestures at our situation.

"Get out of my fucking room," I bite out, but because he's my little brother, he just laughs. This is what I had to deal with growing up, only, it was Dad who'd catch me in the act. I recall the day he caught Rowan on her knees about to suck my dick. The day he took her from me. Camden sure as fuck isn't taking either of these two.

"It's not your room. I couldn't find you, so I figured you'd be in Ethan's room," Camden tells me confidently, and I know I need to talk to him.

"Go to the kitchen. I'll be there in a sec," I tell him, shoving the sheet away, giving my brother an eyeful of my softening dick.

"Oh god, I'm scarred for life," he shouts, spinning on his heel and leaving us to get dressed.

"I'll be back. Sorry about this," I tell Camila. She offers a smile and lazes on the mattress, her eyes sparkling like the ocean just outside the window.

"Go talk to him. We'll be here when you're done." Ethan nods, gesturing to the door. He knows this talk had been coming and that I'd have to do it sooner or later, but he doesn't look concerned. He knows how I feel. Nothing can ever change my love for him.

When I head into the kitchen, I find Camden sitting at the breakfast bar. He's got the business section of the newspaper spread out on the counter, and seems immersed in whatever the fuck he's reading. Beside him is mug of steaming black coffee. How did my baby brother become almost as built and tall as me overnight? It's as if I blinked and the little kid turned into a man.

"You drink coffee now, Cam?" I question, filling my mug. I turn to face my brother and pin him with a stare.

"Yeah, figured I'd make my own since you were having pussy for breakfast." He shrugs, and I can't help cringing at the thought of what he saw.

"Listen—"

"Hey, it's cool. You're an adult, and I'm not Dad. I

don't need to know where your mouth has been." He lifts his gaze from the newspaper to regard me, and something in his confident stare tells me that he'll rule the fucking world one day.

"I know you're not Dad, but I want you to know, this is something I'm going to talk to Hayden and Nix about when I head home soon."

His gaze snaps to mine, searching, asking, but he doesn't voice his concerns. Not that he should have any, but after what he saw, there must be something he wants to ask.

"So, you and Ethan," he finally says, picking up his mug and taking a sip, his eyes never leaving mine.

"Yeah," I respond. The thing about our relationship is Camden never got into my business. He was there for me when I griped about our folks, or Hayden, or even Nixon. Even though I know at times he didn't get why I was angry, he just listened. And that meant more to me than anything ever could.

"I think it's cool. You're all out of the closet and shit," he tells me with an easy shrug. He arches an eyebrow, and I can't stop the laugh that rumbles in my chest.

"I'm not gay, I'm bi," I tell him. "I like girls too."

"So that's what the pretty tan princess was doing sitting on your face." His response makes me cringe. No brother should see something like that.

"Yeah, okay, can you forget it now?"

"Nope. That's what I call blackmail material, bro." He laughs then, a deep, barreling chuckle.

"You're not bothered that I'm in a relationship with Camila and Ethan?" I question, waiting for the confusion, but that's not what I get.

Instead, Camden smiles. "Brock, seriously, don't look for approval. I don't care, as long as you're happy, and from the looks of it, you are."

"You're far too old for your own good, Cam." I snake my arm around his neck, tugging him closer and slamming a kiss on the top of his head like I used to do when we were kids.

"Watch the hair, man," he chides, and I know my little brother will be okay.

Even though our parents are gone, all four of us have gone on to live good lives. We're strong, responsible, and we're slowly finding our way in the world.

As much as I miss my dad, his death brought us closer together—shown us nobody fucks with a Pearson.

"I better pack," Cam tells me. "My flight is in three hours."

"I'll drive you to the airport."

He nods and disappears up the steps. That was easier than I thought it would be. But Camden would always be more understanding than the other two. Now, I need to plan how I'm going to out myself to Nixon and Hayden. Even though I have a feeling they already know, it's up to me to ensure they realize I'm happy.

Ethan and Camila are my new family, my extended family, and I have to show that to both of my other brothers. I'm ready. With a smile, I head up the stairs to find Ethan and Camila lying on his bed.

My best friend's gaze meets mine, and I offer him a nod of approval and a smile. *One down, only two more to go.*

NINETEEN

ETHAN

SHOVING THE DOOR OPEN, I STEP INSIDE AND hear giggling coming from deeper in the house. Brock is right behind me as we make our way into my childhood home. There's a screech from somewhere down the hall, and then Kristyn's gentle voice moments later. The crying from my baby sister is soon quietened. Both emerge from the hallway looking radiant.

"Eeeeee!" Brynn's screech is loud, bouncing around us like surround sound. Thank fuck we're not hungover.

"There's my princess." I scoop her into my arms, offering Krystin a kiss on the cheek.

"How are you, Ethan?" My gorgeous stepmom smiles.

"Good. I missed you." I then focus my attention on

Brynn and spin around. She throws her tiny arms around my neck, holding on for dear life. When I finally stop, I plant a wet kiss on her forehead.

"Eeeeeee!" she squeals at Brock, reaching for him as well.

"Sweet girl," he responds, giving her a kiss on the forehead. Before he pulls away, he gives her a tickle under her arms, which has her wiggling to get free, but I'm far too strong, and soon, there are giggles and squeals that sounds like a fucking Justin Bieber concert.

"Okay, okay." Levi's voice comes from the hallway, and he appears moments later. "Who's killing my little girl?"

If Brynn could talk, I bet she'd rat us out to the old man for tickling her. Her tiny arms reach out to him and I watch as my father chuckles. He takes her from me, and she snuggles into his hold.

"It's okay. I'll sort them out for you." He winks at her, the love shining in his eyes clear. He's happy. I'm happy he's found that again—love, a sense of responsibility he lost when Mom died.

Kristyn waves us into the living room. Her long hair is pinned in a messy bun, and she looks like she's missing out on sleep, but other than that, she's glowing with happiness. It makes me happy to see my father is treating her right—not that I doubted him.

"Boys," she smiles, pulling me into a hug now that I'm free of Brynn, then she moves over to Brock to greet him. "Did you have a good trip?"

"Yeah. Easy flight, no delays, which is always good," I tell her, flopping onto the sofa. She settles beside my dad on the opposite couch while Brock gets comfortable beside me.

"Drinks?" she offers, and I nod. While Kristyn busies herself in the kitchen, I take a moment to watch my dad. He has Brynn in his arms and she's already got droopy eyes. Her excitement is slowly wearing off, and seeing him with her, holding her like I'm certain he held me, makes my heart swell with happiness.

"How's school?" Dad looks up, taking his attention away from Brynn, his dark gaze landing on me.

"Not bad. I'm ready to finish now." My father knows I hate studying. I'd much prefer being on the beach, riding the waves.

"Soon, Ethan, and what about you, Brock?" His tone is serious, commanding, like any father would be, and when I glance at my friend, I know he's thinking about his own dad.

"Acing my exams, Mr. Kingston. I can't wait to get into the working world." Brock is more excited about adulthood than I am. Even though he's a party animal, his marketing degree will be something that will take him far.

"So, you're back to finally tell us all?" Kristyn's smile is beautiful. It lights up her face, and I can see why my father is so enamored with her. She sets the tray of ice cold lemonade I know she made herself on the table.

Grabbing a glass, I fill it and take a long gulp, attempting to calm myself the fuck down. I can't believe I'm worried. "I guess so." I sit forward, nervous energy trailing through me. "I met a girl," I start, noting the shock on both their faces. "Her name is Camila. She's Spanish," I continue. "She, Brock, and I—"

"We're trying something new," Brock finishes for me. I didn't think it would be so difficult finally telling them. Even though they're both pretty open about things, this is not something I ever thought I'd be telling my dad.

"The three of you?" Dad questions. We both nod. "And she knows you're..." he waves his finger between us, and I realize my father doesn't need me to tell him. Even though this probably wasn't how he pictured me living my life, he still loves me. I see it when he looks at me.

"She knows Brock and I are together," I finish for him.

"Good, as long as she accepts it." He sits back, Brynn now passed out in dreamland.

"I'm so happy for you both, and for Camila," Kristyn says, lifting a glass toward us. "You two make a hot couple." She winks slyly, earning her a swat on the thigh from my dad.

"Easy there, Kismet," he coos, low and commanding.

"You're going to tell Hayden and Nixon?" she questions, shaking her head at my father's display of dominance.

"Yeah. It's time. Since we've met Camila, we need to have this out in the open. We'd like to bring her home for Thanksgiving and Christmas, and we'd prefer everyone know before we just lay it on thick."

"That's a good idea," she agrees with Brock.

"You two staying here while you're in town?" Dad asks, sipping the drink then scrunching his face. "This doesn't have any whiskey in it," he tells Kristyn with a grunt.

"Just drink it, Levi," she admonishes him, and I can't help chuckling.

"Just you wait," Dad says, lifting his glass toward me and Brock. "You'll soon be under the thumb as well. Women take over your life when you fall in love." This time, his chest rumbles with a laugh.

"And he wouldn't have it any other way." My stepmother smiles.

Brynn whines loudly into our father's shirt, her tiny hand gripping the material like he's her lifeline. For a long time, I didn't think he was mine. After my mom died, I felt the opposite, but I see now how much he held me afloat.

"You both head to your room. We'll clean up here."

It is late, and I rise, setting the glass down on the tray. That's one thing I have to say about the lady in my dad's life, she's everything he could ever need and more.

"We'll see you in the morning."

"And don't be having loud sex while we're just a few doors down," Levi admonishes as we head down the hall toward my old bedroom.

Shaking my head, I shove open the door, and I'm met with the old me. Everything in here was from my angry teenage years, and now, I have the man I love in here with me. Brock has been in my room so many times before, but never like this. Never as my partner. It's kind of fitting that the first time we fuck is in my childhood bedroom considering it's here where I first felt the stirrings to want such a thing with my best friend.

"This is different."

"It is," I agree. Shutting the door, I step farther into the space as he flops on my bed, his shirt riding up his toned stomach. We'll have to attempt to be quiet.

TWENTY

BROCK

HE CRAWLS OVER ME, DESIRE SWIMMING IN HIS EYES. This is indeed vastly different to how we used to be in this room. This space holds so many memories, and I wouldn't have it any other way. Ethan's mouth closes on mine. His tongue darts out, and mine duels with his once more. The taste of the lemonade mixed with the flavor of the man I've fallen for is heady.

Even though Camila isn't here, I'm still beyond needy for him—for his touch, his body. Every inch of him. We're a mass of arms and legs, attempting to rid ourselves of the material covering what we most want. Skin on skin.

"We're doing this," Ethan grunts, his voice thick with desire, heavy with need. His hands are on me, on my chest. His touch isn't soft and tender like Camila's. It's rough, forceful. Pure sex.

"We are," I agree. I reach out, finding his rigid length, squeezing and stroking him. I can feel his heartbeat in the steel shaft as the blood pulses through it. There's nothing more than animalistic pleasure coursing through my veins when Ethan's hand fists my bare dick and moves up and down, causing my body to burn just for him.

"I need to say something," he pulls away, looking at me as if he's piercing my soul with his dark eyes. I wait, my breathing halted for a moment. To be honest, I'm not sure what he's going to tell me.

Silence.

My heart thuds wildly.

"I'm in fucking love with you," he finally bites out when my hand squeezes his dick as if the words are emblazoned on my chest. He feathers his fingertips over my flesh, then grips my neck, tugging me impossibly closer to him, and this time, I allow him dominance. His thigh nudges between mine, and my hips move involuntarily against him. Needing friction. Humping his fucking leg like an animal.

"Fuck, Ethan," I find words in between our movements, and then he's up on his knees, his cock in my face, and I don't think twice about taking it in my mouth. The salty pre-cum from the tip coats my tongue, and I savor the flavor of him.

Our eyes are locked as I swallow him into my throat, and he curses lowly. At this point, I don't care who hears us. I'm lost to everything this man is. My head bobs up and down, as I lick and suck on his throbbing shaft.

Again and again.

His hand reaches for me, stroking me in time with my movements. I'm so damn close, but I shut my eyes, breathing through the desire, making this last for a long as humanly possible. I need to fuck him. I need to be inside him right the fuck now. I pop my mouth off his cock and glance up.

"I want to be inside you."

He nods, moving to the backpack we brought in from the car, and pulls out a bottle of lube. Seconds later, he's on the bed. He hands me the bottle, and moves on hands and knees in front of me. I move behind him, and soon, the cool liquid is glistening on his skin. I work his body like I would anyone else's. My fingers explore the tight ring of muscle, taunting and teasing him, feeling him tense, then relax, causing low growls to rumble in his chest.

"I'm in fucking love with you too," I bite out as I nudge the head of my dick slowly, inch by torturous inch, into his ass. He's so damn tight, I don't know how I'm going to hold out. Slowly, gently, I sink into him, into my best friend, knowing this is right. I want this. I fucking need this.

Inch by inch, I seat myself fully, balls deep. Ethan's hands fist the sheet, and his body shudders below me, and then I move, pulling my hips back, and sliding into him. Fuck. Pleasure is nothing compared to the euphoria

I feel.

My eyes are shut so tight, I see stars. My fingers dig into his hips, holding him close, needing him closer. I want to climb inside him and know him fully, and I want him to do the same to me. I reach forward, and grip his dick, stroking him, faster and faster as my hips pump into him. It doesn't take long for him to growl out his release, coating my fist. I can't hold back and empty my balls inside Ethan seconds later.

Unrestrained.

This is it.

This is perfect.

This is love.

TWENTY ONE———

E T H A N

THE SUN SHINES THROUGH THE WINDOW. I HEAR Brynn and Kristyn in the kitchen, but I know my father is still asleep. It's a Saturday, and some things never change. Even as I kid, I recall him sleeping in on a weekend.

Brock is still resting beside me. His eyes are closed, and I watch him. It's strange to know we've finally taken that final leap into a real relationship. We've confessed our feelings and we've had sex, just the two of us. It's real now. Not that it wasn't before, but when you tell someone you love them, that's it. And I know once we head back to L.A., it won't be long before I'll be telling Camila the same thing.

"Creeper," Brock mumbles beside me, his voice raspy

with sleep.

"Fuck you," I bite back, only to earn myself a chuckle. A soft knock on the door tells me it's Kristyn. My dad would've just barged in. He's an asshole like that. "Come in," I call to her.

"Morning, boys." She smiles as she steps into the room, kicking the door shut. Dressed in a white flowing dress which makes her look more like a mother than anything I've ever seen her wear. Perhaps my dad is laying down some rules, that makes me laugh. She sets the tray on the desk against the wall then turns to look over at us.

"You brought us coffee? You didn't have to do that," I tell her, scooting up in bed, keeping my crotch covered. I've seen her naked, but she's never had the pleasure of seeing me in the nude and I have to behave since she's married to my dad and technically my mother. That makes me cringe ever so slightly.

"I wanted to. It takes a lot of courage to tell us what you did last night, and I wanted to say I'm proud of you—

both of you." Her gaze flits between us, affection clear in her features.

"Thanks, Kris." I smile.

"Yeah, thank you," Brock responds. "I think telling you is easier than telling my brothers."

She shakes her head. "They'll love you no matter what. You know that, right?"

"I do. I think I'm just nervous about finally telling everyone I'm in love with my best friend," he tells her. My hand finds his and I interlace our fingers. My stepmom smiles, and my heart fills with the happiness living in this house now. Sadness was a permanent resident for so long, but it's filtered out and there are only smiles and love. I finally feel like this is a home again.

"Maaa," Brynn's sweet tone comes from the other side of the door sounding as if she's about to say her first word, but I know it's too soon for that. The sound of her rattle on the floor is a clear indication she's crawling our way, and soon, there's a thump on the door. She's probably trying to push it open, but can't reach the handle and the door is clicked shut. "Eeeeee!" Something I hope will soon be her calling my name is screeched, and I know my dad will be waking up with that.

"Brynn," his deep voice filters through the door, "come here." Little hands and feet patter on the tiles along with the rattle, and she's gone.

"I better go get that man breakfast before he grumbles." Kristyn smiles. "When you're ready, I've made some food, so eat before you head over to Nixon's," she tells us, but she's mainly speaking to Brock, who's so clearly nervous about today.

If he feels anything like I did last night, I doubt eating will do him any good.

"You ready?" I ask him, lifting my coffee as he sips his. Those blue eyes meet mine, and I can see the anxiety coiling in them.

"I think so." He offers me a nervous smile. "I'm not changing my mind, so if you think you're getting rid of me so easily, you're dead wrong," he quips, setting his mug down.

I swallow the last of mine and crawl over him. "I think it's time you showed me just how much you love me," I tell him, my voice a low whisper. He reaches down wordlessly, gripping my bare dick and stroking it 'til I'm solid steel in his hand.

"I think it's time you took what you've been salivating for since we moved in together," he retorts. I chuckle at the cocky asshole.

Lifting onto my knees, I watch him roll over. He's chiseled in all the right places, muscles flexing when he moves. I straddle his waist, my cock nestled on his ass, and I can't help rolling my hips, causing us both to groan.

I reach for the lube and pour a generous amount on the smooth skin, then massage his opening like I did with Camila.

"You ready for this, bro?" I grunt, my fingers teasing him, and he easily moves up onto his knees. When cobalt eyes meet mine, I see the twinkle of need. Working my digits into him, I gently scissor them, ensuring he's calm, loose, and ready for my dick.

"Just fuck me," he bites out, close to losing it.

Nudging his ass, I fist my dick, position the tip, and slowly push into him. The tight ring envelops me, tightening and pulsing. I have to close my eyes to focus. The sensations rocking through me are unlike anything I've ever felt.

Heat spirals through every nerve in my body.

I watch in awe as my dick disappears into his body and tremble as electric shocks race through me. I want to growl, I want to shout out my pleasure, but I don't. Instead, I continue to move inside him, in and out. I mimic his actions from last night, gripping his thick cock, jerking him off while he fists the sheets. Skin slapping, low feral grunts, and pleasure—that's all that exists in this moment, and it doesn't take long for us to find release.

Brock's body shudders below me, and mine follows

suit as I empty myself inside him. I don't want to move. All I need is to stay connected to him for the rest of my life.

TWENTY TWO

B R O C K

NIXON IS AT THE POOL OF HIS LAVISH NEW HOME when I round the corner with Ethan a step behind me. He's lounging in the sun, watching Rowan and Erica in the water, and I can't help smiling. They haven't seen us approach, and I'm tempted to leap in just to splash water all over him, but I refrain.

"Nixon, Ro," I call to them when we're closer. He lifts his head, shoving his sunglasses up, he drags his gaze up to regard me.

"Hey, Brock. I thought you weren't in 'til later?"

"We flew in a day early," I explain. He rises and leans in to pull me into a brotherly hug, slapping my back before shaking Ethan's hand.

"How you doing, Ethan?"

"Good. It's good to be back," my best friend chuckles.

"Oh, Brock." Rowan smiles as she walks toward me. She looks amazing, and I can see why my brother and father fell in love with her. Even though we dated, and I cared deeply about her, I never loved her in the way she deserved. She exits the pool with Erica's hand in hers.

"Brock and Ethan are here," she coos to the little version of her.

"Hi." Erica's beaming smile melts my heart as I scoop her up into my arms.

Rowan places a soft kiss on my cheek and mimics the action for Ethan. Being home again feels good. I should come back more often, and once we're finished with college, I will visit more.

"It's so good to see you both," Rowan beams, happiness shining in her eyes, but I know she must still miss my dad. Every time she looks at Erica, there would be a twinge of sadness, because I feel it.

"It's good to be home," I tell her as Erica's little hand

fists my shirt. She's soaked, but I don't care, just holding her means so much to me. She's part of my dad, and I feel like he's here, looking over us proudly. I swallow the emotion and offer a smile. "Nix, what's up, man?"

"Come inside. I'll grab some beers," he responds with a grin. We follow Nixon into the house, and even though it's not our childhood home, it still reminds me of my younger years and the pool parties we had. The only difference is there are a few toys lying around, which my brother picks up as we stroll farther into the space. That's something that hasn't changed. He's always been meticulous, structured, where I tend to leave my shit all over the place.

As soon as we enter the kitchen, the door opens and Camden saunters in with Hayden—the eldest of the four, and he looks it. All grown up, the spitting image of our father in his suit.

"Brock, Ethan." He smiles, shaking my best friend's hand, then grips my shoulder since I have Erica on my lap. She silently watches us with those curious eyes.

"How's business?" I question, and the look on Hayden's face says it all.

"Good. Living the life Dad intended," he informs me coolly. He wanted me beside him at Four Fathers Freight, but over time, he came to terms it wasn't going to happen.

"I'm sure he's proud of you," I tell him, earning a nod.

"How's the beautiful señorita?" Camden pipes up, a smarmy grin on his face. *Asshole*. Pinning him with a warning glare, I shake my head.

"Señorita?" Ro questions. "Is there a girl we don't know about?"

"Yeah, she's gorgeous." My little brother decides to throw me right in the deep end before I can respond.

"Thanks, Cam," I roll my eyes in frustration at my youngest brother offering up the news that I wanted to tell them.

Hayden's ears perk up at this. He leans forward, his elbows on the breakfast bar.

"We came home to talk to everyone," I start, glancing back at Ethan for a moment, then allowing my gaze to fall on each of my brothers, then Rowan. "Camila is my girlfriend." My voice is wary, and I wait for a second before continuing. "And Ethan and I..." I allow my words to taper off, hoping they'll figure it out, but not one of them moves. When I look at Camden, he raises an eyebrow, and his lips quirk with a barely hidden smile.

"Yeah?"

"Well, Ethan, Camila, and I...we're in a relationship," I finally spit out.

A soft gasp from Rowan has me dragging my eyes to hers. "That's awesome! I'm so happy for you!" She leaps from the chair, inadvertently waking Erica, who's now excitedly bouncing in my lap seeing her mother making her way over to us. Rowan wraps her arms around me in a motherly hug, planting a kiss on my cheek.

"I knew it," Nix boasts with a smile. "I fucking knew you and Ethan were a thing." There's no anger, no judgment, just pure happiness on his face. Nixon has always been the serious one, a loner, but since he's been with Rowan, something in him has changed, but only slightly.

I turn my gaze to Hayden, waiting for him to say something, anything. But he just sits there for a moment before he finally smirks. "A true fucking Pearson," he says. "Dad would've been proud that you snagged yourself two amazing people to share your life with."

My chest aches at his words. Sadness races through me, and I have to blink back the tears. I fucking miss Eric Pearson, the asshole he was, and wish every day he was still here.

"Thanks, guys, and thank you, Ro."

"I'm so glad that's outta the bag," Cam chuckles. He lifts a glass of lemonade to his lips and takes a long gulp. When he sets it down, everyone's eyes are on him. "What? I can keep a secret." This time, he offers us a wink that makes us all laugh.

I glance at Ethan, who's smiling widely. Rowan is hugging him, but his eyes are on me.

"So, when do we get to meet Camila?" Hayden questions, grabbing a beer from the fridge.

"Soon. We wanted to do this first, but she'll come home with us for Thanksgiving," I tell him. I want her to meet the family, to meet the Pearsons and the Kingstons, because soon, she'll be a part of us. Let's just hope we don't scare her away.

TWENTY THREE——

C A M I L A

ONE MONTH LATER

SINCE THEY'VE BEEN HOME, IT'S BEEN A WHIRLWIND of school, spending time in the ocean with my surfboard, and being in my new home. Ethan and Brock returned from their vacation to ask me to move in with them. Even though we're taking it slow, the past month has been amazing.

My father was unsure at first, but when he met the boys, he could tell how much they cared about me. There wasn't anything he could fault them on, and trust me, he tried really hard to.

Santiago Alvaro is not an easy man to please, but with Brock and Ethan's connections to Four Fathers

Freight, he was visibly interested in doing business with Hayden and Levi. The sun is already high in the clear blue sky and there isn't a cloud in sight as I watch Ethan and Brock fight it out on the waves. They're both on their surfboards, and I settle onto one of the patio chairs to watch my two men enjoy themselves.

I never thought being in a relationship with them would be so fulfilling. Growing up, it was drilled into me to find a nice Spanish boy, get married, and have a few kids, so to me, this is far outside the norm. They give me everything I need and more—so much more.

Watching them together, so in love, only makes me love them more. We haven't said it yet, but I know soon enough, those words will slip from my lips and I'll confess my feelings to them. I love them both in their uniqueness. Brock, the cocky, blue-eyed, rough-around-the-edges one, and Ethan, the brown-eyed, sweet talker.

So different in their personas, but so similar in the way they love me. And I know they do. I see it in their actions, in the way they look at me, touch me, and the way we make love.

They're walking toward the apartment, both sets of eyes on me, and I offer them a wave. Moments later, the front door opens and clicks shut.

"Good morning, sweetheart," Ethan greets, placing a soft kiss on my cheek, his hair still dripping. It's almost shoulder-length now, and I can tangle my fingers through it while his head is between my legs.

"Did you have a good surf?"

"Yeah," Brock responds as he kisses my forehead. "There was one fucker of a wave that knocked me on my ass," he tells me, flopping into the chair opposite me. His blue eyes are even more piercing in the sunlight.

"I missed it," I pout, laughing when he flips me the bird. What I love most about them is they don't treat me like a fragile little girl. I'm their equal. Even with all their alpha macho actions, they make me feel like one of them. They respect my opinion.

"What are we doing today?" Brock questions, glancing between the two of us. It's only eight in the morning, and I planned on lazing around and doing nothing today.

"We could..." Ethan's voice lowers to a whisper, and both sets of eyes are on me. There's nothing innocent in either one.

"What?"

"Just thinking," Brock says.

Ethan winks. "About you."

"Naked," his best friend finishes.

"Oh? And what would happen if I were?" I ask coyly, reaching for the buttons of one of Brock's dress shirts, my fingers deftly undoing them one by one, allowing it to fall open. When I woke up this morning in an empty bed, I didn't bother getting dressed, just threw a shirt on.

"We'd have to take you into the living room, because we wouldn't want anyone seeing you, or hearing you scream our names." Brock's voice is filled with heated confidence.

"And then?" I ask, rising from my chair. Turning toward the apartment, I slip the material over my shoulders and let it fall to the floor.

Two deep growls rumble from behind me, and I can't help a squeal when arms wrap around my waist. Ethan. He lifts me up and stalks indoors until I'm at the large sofa. When he sets me down, his mouth crashes to mine in a kiss so hungry and feral, it steals my breath.

"Sit," he orders as he pulls away. Brock is behind me on the plush cushions, stroking himself through his shorts.

I settle on Brock's lap, my back to his front. Ethan positions my feet, one on either side of Brock's legs, opening me to him. He drops his head between my thighs, and his hot tongue laps at my core, licking and suckling on my clit.

I look down to meet those dark eyes that peek up at me as he devours me. This is how I wake up every morning, either blue or brown eyes watching me.

"Oh, oh, God," I cry out when Ethan dips two fingers into me and crooks them to hit that spot inside me that has my toes curling and my hips rolling against him, riding his face like I would either of their cocks. Brock's fingers tease and taunt my nipples, and I can't hold back my release.

Pleasure zips through every inch of my body. My nerves are alight, and my blood is hot, burning through me. Everything becomes white noise when Ethan frees his best friend's cock and nudges it against my pussy.

"Ride him," he orders, his mouth working Brock's cock and my pussy. The sight is so ilicit, I slide down on the thick erection, opening myself further, stretching me to the point of pain, but it's far from agony, it's pure bliss.

My body rises and falls as I bounce on his cock like a woman possessed. I'm needy and dripping on the tongue of the man I love while being impaled by the other.

Three hearts.

Three souls.

One forever.

"I love you both," I cry out as my body pulses and I soak both men in my juices. Ethan smirks at me after he drinks every drop.

"We love you too," Brock confirms. Ethan nods, and I'm lost to euphoria.

EPILOGUE

ETHAN

IT'S ALWAYS JUST BEEN MY DAD AND ME. NO ONE ELSE could replace the empty space my mother left. It was our world, and he taught me how to survive in it. I thought I'd become cold, and for a while, I was.

I didn't think about loving someone else.

I never saw myself finding a permanent sense of happiness. It was too far-fetched, but I was just short-sighted. My forever is not with one, but two hearts.

They're in the water, both on their surfboards, and I watch her for a moment. Camila walked into our lives when we needed her. Her long, flowing hair loose as it hangs down her back, stopping just above her pert little ass. Her tiny pink bikini covers her, barely, but she's feisty and won't allow us to tell her what she's not allowed to wear.

Her smile is bright as she looks over at my best friend. And that's what I love about her. That smile. Those eyes. And her strong personality.

Brock always tells me I saved him, but he doesn't realize just how much he saved me. How he made me fall when it was the last thing on my mind. It wasn't that *knowing* kind, where your eyes meet and that's it. No, we gradually become each other's board, weathering the waves together.

We face a new life now. Three of us. A forever with three hearts that not only love unconditionally, but three bodies that experience pleasure in a way two people can ever come close to. Perhaps I'm biased. Yes, I believe I am.

My gaze flits to him—Brock Pearson. His dark hair is wet, shining in the sunlight as he looks over at Camila— our girl. His body is filling out, toned, tan, mine.

It's not conventional.

It's not your everyday type of romance.

But when the apple doesn't fall far from the tree, how could Brock and I ever have anything less than unique?

B R O C K

It's Ethan's birthday today. I wanted to do something special—to offer him a gift he'll never forget because he gave me something I will always remember. He gave me my life back. When my heart stopped beating that day, after my father get shot, it was Ethan who put me back together.

I never saw myself in a normal relationship. If I'm being honest, I never saw myself as a forever type of guy. I wanted to be the carefree playboy my father was. He was always my role model, and even though I spent the better part of my time inside every hot girl I could, there was always him.

Ethan was the one person who was a constant. I needed him to breathe, to feel, to experience things I never thought possible. I wasn't expecting to fall in love with my best friend. It just happened. It was the most normal thing to finally feel his lips on mine, his strong hands gripping me, pulling me closer.

And even though we've found love with each other, we've found a third heart to love.

Camila.

Her strength, tenacity, and those incredible fucking curves make me want to be inside her all the time. But even though the physical is so perfect, what makes her so alluring is the fire that burns in her eyes.

She doesn't take our shit. She calls us out and makes us accountable when we need it. Which we do at times.

The door opens, and she strolls in.

"Hey." Her greeting is accompanied by a small smile.

"Hey, baby girl," I respond, watching her set the book bag down on the floor. She heads my way to plant a kiss on my lips. Hers mold to mine, as if they were always meant to be there. "So, I've been thinking," I whisper, hoping Ethan doesn't come home yet. If he overhears my plan, it will spoil the surprise. "Tonight, we should head out for a special dinner."

"Oh?" She tips her head to the side as she straddles me. "For Ethan's birthday?"

Nodding, I murmur along her lips, "Yes, and I want you in that red dress."

"I think I can manage that." Her smile is bright.

"Go. We'll leave as soon as he gets home and changes. It shouldn't be too much longer." I slap her on the ass, and she squeals, which doesn't help the hardening of my dick.

I watch her scurry down the hall to the bedroom we all share. Smiling, I turn to my computer and finish up my work. Tonight, I'll finally cement our relationship.

CAMILA

Dinner was incredible. Both guys look like they just walked off the pages of a GQ magazine. Brock dressed in a blue shirt that matches his eyes, and black suit pants, and Ethan's in a gray shirt and black pants. No ties, but with the dress I wore, it matches up.

Brock bought it for me a week ago. The plunging back is revealing, but the front only offers a small glimpse of my cleavage. Thin spaghetti straps sparkle along my shoulders, and the hem stops mid-thigh. It's sexy, yet elegant.

"I wanted to celebrate tonight," Brock starts, lifting the champagne flute the waiter filled only moments ago. I lift mine, and Ethan follows suit. "You're both incredibly special to me, and of course, tonight is Ethan's birthday."

We clink our glasses, and I give one of my men a kiss on the mouth. His lips, full and soft, feel warm against mine.

"So," Brock continues, "in honor of this special evening, I need to say something sappy," he chuckles. "I don't do that often, so bear with me."

"Dude," Ethan starts with a smile, "no need to be emotional, you know I love you."

"That's why I need to say this. So shut up and listen." Brock rolls his eyes, and I laugh at both of them acting all alpha while still showing how much they care. "I want us to be a forever. To have our own family one day."

"We will." My assurance makes him smile that grin that always makes me stomach flutter wildly when he gifts it. Brock Pearson is good looking, devastatingly so, and I can't believe he loves me. I'm the shy girl from a strict family that couldn't understand my choice to live with them, but slowly, they're coming to accept this is our love and life.

It's not conventional, it's not something you'll hear about every day, but it's real, and it's mine.

Brock sets two boxes on the table, one in front of me, and one before Ethan. They match, both a deep blue velvet. My heart speeds up, leaping into my throat.

"Open them." He gestures to the objects with his chin.

I snap mine open, and there, on a sleek silver necklace,

is a pendant—a locket. When I click it open, inside is a photo of me sandwiched between both men. We're on the beach, it was our first surf date after they came out to the Pearson family, along with Levi and Kristyn and soon I'll be there alongside them at the special occasions as part of the family.

"It's beautiful."

"You're beautiful," both guys respond in unison, and we all laugh.

Ethan snaps his box open, and there on the velvet is a chain—thicker and wider than my necklace—but this has a pocket watch on it. When he taps the lock, it opens to the same photo in my locket.

"It's us. Happy. Forever. And when the time is right, we'll make it official. We're not sure how, but with time, it will come to us."

My heart is filled with love and affection. I still sometimes wonder how this will work, and even though not everyone knows about the three of us, we don't hide the fact that we're together. There isn't any room in my life for judgment. It may not be conventional, but it's mine. It's real. There's love between us that nobody can tear apart.

I smile as Brock fastens the chain around my neck. It's perfect, dainty, but it holds a promise of everything I never thought I needed that's become all I ever wanted— to be accepted for who I am, for the real me I've always hidden from my family.

The two boys kiss, their tongues tangling. The sight is erotic, sensual, and I can't tell what makes me hotter— watching them or them focusing on me.

"Don't just sit there." Ethan tugs me closer, and I grip them through their clothes.

"Let's play."

ENJOYED THIS BOOK?
MEET THE OTHER SONS

Four Sons Series by bestselling authors

J.D. Hollyfield, Dani René,

K Webster, and Ker Dukey

Four genres.

Four bestselling authors.

Four different stories.

Four weeks.

One intense, sexy,

thrilling ride from beginning to end!

*** This series should be read in order to understand the plot.***

Who's the daddy now?

NIXON

KER DUKEY

A FOUR SONS STORY
There's a new sheriff in town...
HAYDEN
J.D. HOLLYFIELD

OTHER BOOKS IN THE
FOUR SONS SERIES

HAYDEN

BY JD HOLLYFIELD

I am a hothead, a wild card, and son to a murdered man.
I crave the things I can't have and don't want the things
I can.

Now, I'm left to pick up the pieces—stitch our family
back together with a damaged thread.
This isn't the life I envisioned. And to make matters
worse, the women in our lives are testing the strength of
our brotherhood.

My name is Hayden Pearson.

I am the eldest—a protective, but vindictive son.
People may think I'm too young to fill our father's shoes,
but it won't stop me from proving them all wrong.

*** *This series should be read in order to understand the plot.* ***

A ring won't stop
the determined…

CAMDEN

K WEBSTER

OTHER BOOKS IN THE
FOUR SONS SERIES

CAMDEN
BY K WEBSTER

I am intelligent, unassuming,
and the son of two murdered parents.
I'm calculating, damaged, and seek revenge.

I'll do whatever it takes to further my agenda, even if it
means seducing my way into a bed I don't belong.
Anything to make the ones who've hurt me pay.

My name is Camden Pearson.

I am focused, fierce, and power-hungry.
The youngest of four brothers.
People assume I'm the baby, but I grew up a long time
ago.

This series should be read in order to understand the plot.

ACKNOWLEDGMENTS

Firstly, thank you to Kristi for inviting me on this journey. She's not only an amazing author herself, she's a wonderful friend.

To Monica who tirelessly worked out all the timelines and polished up Brock and Ethan, thank you lady! You rock!!

I've had so much fun tipping my toe into unchartered waters with these three beautiful characters. It's been so much fun to write Brock and Ethan, and introducing Camila to the family.

Thank you to the three ladies who helped BETA this

chapter by chapter, begging for more each time I hadn't updated the document, Alicia, Allyson, and Cat—you three ladies have been nothing short of amazing!

A huge thanks to my my Angels street team—Tre, Sheena, Sarah, Lisa, Caroline, TJ, Hayfaah, Joy, Cinders, Fran, Erin, Tanya—thank you for pimping my work EVERYWHERE. You ladies rock!!

My reader group, The Darklings, as always, you're the only place I know I'll find like-minded ladies and a handful of gents who will have a laugh without drama. The group has grown so much and I'm excited for the future! Thank you for being there.

To all my author colleagues, thank you for always sharing, commenting, and supporting me. I appreciate every one of you. Having a support system is important and you ladies provide that and so much more.

Readers and bloggers, from the bottom of my little black heart, THANK YOU. All you do for us authors is incredible. Reading and reviewing is demanding on your own time and you do it with a smile. Thank you so, so much. You are valued and appreciated for taking time out to show us so much love.

If you enjoyed this story, please consider leaving a review. I'd love you forever. (Even though I already do!)

ABOUT DANI RENÉ

Dani is an international bestselling author and proud member of the Romance Writer's Organization of South Africa (ROSA) and the Romance Writer's of America (RWA).

A fan of dark romance that grabs you by the throat and doesn't let go. It's from this passion that her writing has evolved from sweet and romantic, to dark and delicious. It's in this world she's found her calling, growing from strength to strength and hitting her stride.

On a daily basis, she has a few hundred characters, storylines, and ideas floating around in her head. From the feisty heroines she delivers to the dark, dominant alphas that grace the pages of her books, she promises light in a world filled with danger and darkness.

She has a healthy addiction to reading, TV series, music, tattoos, chocolate, and ice cream.

STALK LINKS

Do you follow me?

If not, head over to any of the below links,

I love to hear from my readers!

FB Group: Dani's Darklings

IG: @danireneauthor

FB Page: DaniReneAuthor

GR: Dani René

Amazon: Dani René

Newsletter: http://bit.ly/2sAy5dU

BookBub: Dani René

Twitter: @DaniReneAuthor

OTHER BOOKS

Broken Series

Broken by Desire

Shattered by Love

The Backstage Series

Between Love & Fire

Between Lust & Tears

Between Want & Fear

Forbidden Series

From the Ashes - A Prequel

Crave (Book #1)

Covet (Book #2)

Stand Alones

Ace of Harts

Love Beyond Words

CUFFED

Fragile Innocence (A dark ménage romance)